Seasons of Affection

Jim Shields

Book Reality

Helping Writers Become Independent Authors

Cover Design by Luke Buxton | www.lukebuxton.com

Sources:
From In Memoriam, Tennyson, Alfred, Oxford Library of English Poetry Vol. III, 1986, Oxford University Press: Oxford.
Mill Street – Clifford, John, The Corran - Journal of Larne and District Folklore Society 1988-1990. U/A Lar 394.6: Larne
Walden, or Life in the Woods, Thoreau, Henry David, 1854, Ticknor and Fields: Boston
The Road not Taken, Frost, Robert, The Poetry Foundation, retrieved 2022, https://www.poetryfoundation.org/poems/44272/the-road-not-taken

To Eileen and to all who generously share

their discernment and wisdom

And to all who inform my understanding of compassion

All author royalties for this book will be donated to the
Ukrainian International Appeal Fund.

Erratum:
page 104:
Last line;
for "2014"
read "1914"

Table of Contents:

For my wife, Annette

and our children,

Paul, Grainne, Gregory, Mary and Gavin

who everyday are my motivation.

The Gathering

The year is 2019. Harry and Martha, octogenarians, had celebrated their diamond wedding anniversary five years earlier; a special occasion they'd spent months preparing for. Unfortunately, some of their family hadn't been able to attend and so, this coming Christmas would be the first time in two decades that they would have all their children back in the home where they were born and reared.

Martha and Harry married when they were in their early twenties. It was an ordinary marriage by any standards, nothing spectacular, black and white regular. Starting their journey through life, third class, on society's travellator. Busy raising their five children, they transitioned into middle age without discernment. Time had passed breathtakingly fast, and that they weren't young anymore didn't bother them. Sprightly, ailment free and physically fit, they looked forward to – *the gathering* – with mounting anticipation.

Everything was readied, but Martha was anxious; she couldn't help it. Weekly phone calls to her offspring had become ritualistic. She wanted everyone to feel at home, relaxed, at ease, especially the grandchildren, hoping they would forge lasting relationships. Eager to please, everything had to be welcoming.

Harry could feel her angst beginning to sizzle as, day by day, Christmas came closer. Easy-going by nature, Harry was more laid back.

"We've done the best we could to make everyone welcome; if we've overlooked something, we'll just have to pull together and make the best of it," he insisted.

Martha fussed with the this's and that's – until the first of their gathering presented at her front door. It was the week before Christmas when the family began arriving. With their five children, attendant spouses and grandchildren, it made for ten adults and thirteen children coming in from all over the world. Harry did the airport pickups while Martha waited expectantly, table set, refreshments readied.

Deidre, her husband Owen and three children, were the first arrivals. They drove from Edinburgh to Cairnryan to make the short sea crossing to Northern Ireland by ferry. Disembarking, in familiar territory, they didn't need directions. Being first to arrive satisfied Deidre's innate need to assist her mother, even though she knew her mother didn't require assistance. Owen, a graphic designer by profession, dutifully shared the burden of Deidre's desire. He was a tall, lean, muscular man with brown eyes and dark curly hair; he spoke like Sean Connery. Martha liked the sound of his voice. Being quietly disposed, he was prone to letting his imagination distil, filter and visually formulate concepts that injected life and energy into client's dry wordy briefs.

Sean, his wife Denise and their four children were the next arrivals. It was an early pick up for Harry. Sean, a carpenter, had gone to New Zealand to work; met Denise, fell in love, married and settled in Christchurch. The first time Sean saw Denise, he was smitten. He couldn't help himself. There was nothing remarkable about Denise; but she was much more than the sum of her features; her attraction was her composition. It was something Sean realised when they first met. Denise, a teacher, loved children. Blessed with an endearing personality, she eagerly looked forward to *the gathering* in Sean's birthplace and the opportunity to explore his childhood haunts and meet some of the pals he often fondly mentioned.

The same day, late in the afternoon, Eamon, his wife Florence and their two children arrived from the USA. Eamon, a plumber, was on holiday in California when offered a job. The money was too good to refuse. Then Eamon started his own business, diversifying into property development as his plumbing business grew. He had hired Florence, a landscape architect, to work on one of his projects. She was easy to work with, and Eamon liked her. As the project progressed, he felt drawn towards her. At first, it was a distraction; in her company his mind wasn't on his work, but as her attraction grew he felt more at ease in her presence. There was an elegance about her and her work that Eamon admired. She was alluring, good-looking, and easy company; by the time Eamon realised he was in love, he discovered Florence was too.

Frank, his wife Coralie, and their two children, the French connection, presented themselves at Martha's front door the following day. Coralie, petite, luminous dark skin, ash blonde hair, dressed with casual flamboyance, bounced down the path on her new sneakers to greet Martha and Harry with outstretched open arms. Frank had met Coralie when he was teaching at Sorbonne University in Paris. Coralie exuded in every way the self-confidence of a professional artist. Her catchphrase Harry would remember because he'd hear it so often during *the gathering* was, *C'est comme Ca*. Harry had to ask what it meant – it's like that – or as Harry chose to remember it – life's like that.

The last to arrive to complete *the gathering* was Peter, his wife Gabriela and their three children. When Harry first saw Gabriela, he thought she was everything a Goddess should be. He always thought the lyrics of a Spanish song he had once heard, Al Andalus, personified Gabriela completely. Her looks did indeed combine cultures and her charm stole your soul.

Peter, an architect, met Gabriela when working in Granada. A final year student, she was trying to supplement her tuition fees busking in the square.

By any stretch of one's imagination, *the gathering* was a family melting pot, in which different cultures, mixing, mingling and blending, assimilated into a cohesive whole. A microcosm of what the world could be.

The family home, a three-story semi-detached house on Chaine Memorial Road, in the harbour town of Larne, gateway to the Glens of Antrim in the north of Ireland, had a roof space conversion and was big enough to accommodate everyone – they hoped. But it was a bit of a tight squeeze. Once the dust settled; a make-do, put-up-with, accept it for what it is, happy holiday attitude emerged, which was greatly enhanced when the grandchildren took to their inflatable mattress beds like ducks to water. Happily, everyone was satisfied. The youngest grandchildren viewed the inflatable beds as bouncy playthings at first. The house, filling with new arrivals, quivered in expectation. It was like a beehive in mid-summer.

The weather being kind, the grandchildren, of mixed ages and genders, quickly and easily making friends, set about familiarising themselves with their new surroundings. They thoroughly explored every nook and cranny inside the old house until curiosity forced them outdoors. Like cats hunting mice, they were in, through and out of the sheds. The greenhouse somehow survived unscathed. There wasn't a tree they didn't climb

4

or a gate they didn't swing on. Watching their exploratory activities, through the kitchen window, Harry musingly remarked, "It's great to hear the sound of children about the house again. Isn't it Martha?"

Without lifting her head from the kitchen sink, Martha smiling sighed, "You think so. It's early days yet, dear."

Outside, the sound of happy noises continued unabated. There were disagreements, disputes, minor accidents, scrapes and bruises, all part and parcel of children at play. Harry had seen it all before. In readiness for their stay, he had secured everything that, he thought, could present a danger: sharp tools, pesticides, medicines and the like. But he couldn't anticipate all their tomfoolery. Children are like that, irrepressible.

They were playing a ball game in the garden one day; noisy rumbustious play. The sudden silence alerted Harry that something was amiss. He went to investigate. Tommy, the eldest child, was standing on the flat roof of the garden shed. He had climbed onto it, with the aid of a refuse bin and a stool, purloined to retrieve the wayward ball. It lay tantalising close to Tommy, in the middle of the roof. Harry knew the roof wouldn't take Tommy's weight if he stepped towards the ball. Tommy stood, innocently looking down at Harry. Capturing his gaze, Harry held it, casually walking towards the child, talking all the while in a calm, soft voice. He didn't want Tommy to look away, feeling guilty, frightened or threatened. The roof was corrugated asbestos sheeting. *You wouldn't be allowed to build that now,* Harry thought, still talking slowly, calmingly, his eyes fixed on Tommy's. If the child were to take another step on the roof, he would fall through it, onto goodness knows what lay below. *Oh God, I should have replaced that roof long ago. Too late now, Harry,* he thought, focusing on Tommy.

Still calmly engaging the child, Harry moved closer. Retrieving the stool and standing on it, he reached out and plucked the child off the roof, away from danger. Harry stood rooted on the spot, clasping Tommy to his chest. The heart he felt pounding wasn't his grandson's. It was his. Breathlessly he whispered in Tommy's ear, 'Please don't ever go up there again, Tommy son; it's too dangerous. Promise me, please, Tommy?"

Setting Tommy on the ground, Harry, with the aid of a step ladder and long-handled brush, fetched the ball off the roof. Ball in hand, children around him, Harry without reproach cautioned them about unseen dangers when playing in unfamiliar places.

"Listen, everyone, be careful. If you think of doing something that might be difficult or dangerous, ask Tommy about it, he's the eldest, and if he's not around, ask me or any adult. Okay?"

Thirteen pairs of eyes innocently gazed up at Harry. Disarmed, Harry threw the ball into the garden and watched them scampering after it. As they played he did another tour around the outhouses and gardens, looking for hazards he may have missed. When he recounted the incident, Coralie shrugged, saying, "*C'est comme Ca.*"

Christmas Eve morning eased into the afternoon. Anticipation slowly filtered through the house. Excitement rippled among the children; they knew that Santa was on his way. Early in the afternoon, Harry gathered the children to help prepare for Father Christmas's much-anticipated annual visit. Sheepishly, in single file, they followed him into the spacious family room. Standing them in a semi-circle around the inglenook fireplace, Harry explained that they would have to remove the fire grate piece by piece and put them out of Father Christmas's way so that he wouldn't trip over them and hurt himself.

"We don't want that to happen now. Do we?"

"No," they chorused in unison.

"Certainly not, otherwise he might not be generous tonight," Harry cautioned. "The hearth has to be swept clean, spotlessly clean so that Father Christmas will have somewhere nice and clean to put his feet when he comes down the chimney. If he leaves here with dirty boots, your Granny will be furious. The folk next door will know our hearth wasn't clean. People will talk. Won't they?"

Kneeling in the inglenook, looking over his shoulder, Harry saw twenty-six legs and thirteen faces with twenty-six wide-open eyes fixed on him.

"He comes down this chimney with presents for you, right?" Harry asked. "You wouldn't want him to leave his dirty boot prints all over the floor, would you? What would your Granny say?"

"No." Thirteen heads solemnly shook from side to side.

With the fire grate removed, placed out of Santa's way, and the hearth swept clean, Harry sent the children to wash their hands before proceeding with the next task.

"Next, the Christmas tree," Harry said, pointing to the big tree in the corner of the room. "It needs a few more decorations. There's a box of stuff in the corner; choose some things and finish decorating the tree."

Eagerly they scattered like rabbits. It took a while. Eventually, when finished and everything tidied up, Harry said, "I almost forgot! There's something else we must do."

The children looked at him bemused.

"We must leave refreshments for Father Christmas before we go to bed tonight; he'll be tired, won't he? It's hard work, you know, delivering presents to everyone."

"Yes," they nodded, like life-size automatons.

"Well, what do you think he would like?" Harry asked.

After many varied suggestions, the consensus eventually reached was mince pies, ginger ale and chocolate. Harry chose not to invite ideas for reindeer refreshments. The room readied for their visitor; they stood in silence for a moment, thoughts and hopes registering on their innocent faces. Then drawing the window curtains, Harry gently ushered them out and locked the door.

"We won't disturb Father Christmas when he's about his work now. Will we?" Harry whispered. Their awed silence spoke volumes.

Everything was readied for the Eve of Christmas supper. An adjoining room catered for the overspill from the dining room. Dining room lights dimmed; Martha always liked to create an atmosphere. The coloured candles were lit with a flourish, releasing their warm, comforting glow. Supper was underway without fuss. It was a light supper; potato and leek soup, gratins of fresh smoked salmon with beetroot and dill, platters of crudités with assorted dips and for afters, homemade sticky toffee pudding.

Conversation flowed around the table, laughter blending with supper noises. The overspill room emitted happy noises, too – most of the time. Occasionally a parent settled some internecine dispute, fortunately, without recourse to force of arms.

With the debris of supper cleared away, conversation hushed, the house quietened, filling with anxious expectation. Younger children fought a losing battle with sleep; others went to bed hoping that night would pass quickly. Empty stockings, awaiting filling, lay in hope around the inflatables. The night was deepening, Harry, quietly, in the family room with an old boot, made imprints on soot, liberally dusted on the hearth. Santa's presents quickly and quietly ferried in were piled under the Christmas tree. Everything readied for the morning, Harry locked the door.

Parents filled stockings of hope as children slept. With everything ready for the chaos of the morning to come, they raised glasses as the clock struck twelve and toasted the dawning of Christmas day. Harry thought he saw the glimmer of a tear in Martha's eyes. He dabbed his eyes with a handkerchief, thinking *joy to the world.*

The rising sun was urging the darkness of the night to yield when clamorous children, discovering that Father Christmas had come, roused the household. Bleary-eyed parents unceremoniously awakened, rushed to share in the feverish excitement swirling through the house. At the family room door, Harry poised, key in hand, waited as the children swarmed around until all had gathered and settled before he tantalisingly turned the key and eased the door open. The children rushed in like a tidal wave and there was no containing them. They halted abruptly, momentarily overwhelmed when they saw the black footprints on the hearth and floor.

"Look, what did I tell you? The people next door didn't clean their chimney! They'll be lucky if Father Christmas left them anything. But he liked your preparations; the refreshments are gone." Harry exclaimed,

"He's come, Father Christmas has come, he's come," thirteen voices chorused.

Father Christmas's footprints led all eyes towards the Christmas tree and what lay heaped underneath.

Averting chaos, Martha exercising matriarchal authority, organised the retrieval of Santa's presents from under the Christmas tree. Tentatively the youngest child edged towards the bundles under the Christmas tree, found its treasure trove, turned and ran back into the arms of mother. The pace quickened with age as excitement surged. In minutes the thirteen had secured their bundles, leaving the floor beneath the Christmas tree looking pillaged.

Presents unceremoniously unwrapped, exposing what Santa Claus had brought, produced squeals of delight. The oh's and ah's and the 'look what I've got's' and the 'what have you got's?' 'It's just what I wanted,' echoed around the room with adults vicariously sharing their children's joy. Happy sounds filled the old house to its rafters. Wee Jimmy's parents searched for the battery he had lost, eventually finding it under a chair. Annie's doll's dislocated arm needed fixing and Harry was able to supply batteries for those not included with various electronic games.

Parents helped with things that needed assembling. Harry eagerly got involved too, the child in him shining through. There were games to enjoy, puzzles to solve, books to read, things to explore, and much more. It was a joyous, noisy, exciting, exhilarating family Christmas morning. No one wanted breakfast, but the adults welcomed the mid-morning refreshment.

Harry watching everything, smiled inwardly, remembering the Christmas he found Santa's presents in the glory hole under the stairs. His mother had forgotten to lock the door. He didn't believe in Santa after that. The game was up. He was ten. *When and how will my grandchildren learn the truth about Santa,* he wondered.

Christmas morning weather was vibrantly sharp. Those gifted a bicycle, tricycle, pedal-powered car or football gear, eagerly ventured outdoors. Exhaled breath visibly plumed from open mouths into the crisp morning air. The early morning initial excitement yielded to earnest pursuits. Indoors, the younger children played quietly together, sharing their toys, making stories. Slowly everything quietened.

Unnoticed, preparations for Christmas day lunch, always a late afternoon occasion, were quietly underway. With much of the prepping already done, those with assigned tasks went about their work under Martha's maternal eye. Those without culinary chores were not left idle; they had the challenging duty of shepherding high-spirited, exuberant children until lunchtime. Eamon was called upon to use his plumbing skills to fix a misbehaving ball cock in the water cistern tucked away in the roof space.

Aromas of Christmas lunch in preparation slowly drifted through the house as the Aga cooker laboured at utmost capacity. Whiffs of roasting turkey shrouded in streaky bacon and clove-studded baking ham combined with those of warm cranberry sauce, ginger, cloves, cinnamon, and nutmeg with the distinctive aroma of vegetable broth permeating every nook and cranny.

The lunch was a triumph without pomp and ceremony. An aperitif of chilled sparkling wine greeted adults with soft drinks of choice for children. The traditional starter of vegetable broth waited in its ceramic tureen in the centre of the table until everyone was seated. When Martha removed the tureen top, the room was filled with the aromatic freshness of soft herbs. The accompaniment for the vegetable broth was humble homemade wheaten bread with butter – always a Martha's must. The children in the overflow room were catered for; their every need was attended to by a posse of parent-waiters. – It was that kind of carefree, jolly celebration.

For the main event, everyone gathered around the dining table. Martha glided into the room, an aura of calmness about her. The tiny birthmark on one side of her Adam's apple moved when she spoke. It was eye-catching. Parents lifted younger children to see the enormous browned turkey and crackling covered ham paraded in and ceremoniously placed on the centre of the table, followed by dishes of mashed potatoes and golden brown roasties. Platters of roasted parsnips, carrots and sprouts also graced the table. Then with everything readied, Martha carved and served the turkey and Harry likewise the ham.

With plated turkey and ham passed around, self-service was the order of the day. There was much toing and froing and the passing of this and that, but soon everything settled. The succulent turkey, cranberry sauce, sage and onion stuffing, and baby sausages were delicious. Everyone tucked in with full-bodied red wine, white for those who preferred it, and soft drinks for the children. Mutterings of 'delicious' circulated the table, accompanied by sighs of unrestrained satisfaction.

Desert arrived at the table with a flourish. Martha's speciality, homemade apple cake. Three of them, made with three different types of apple, baked in a shortcrust pastry and topped with rich custard. The *'Oliver Twists'* were not denied more.

It was early evening before the debris of lunch was cleared away. The adults gathered in the family room, settling around the open fire. The children amused themselves, and Harry performed the role of a sommelier with great aplomb, serving drinks from various bottles on a side table. Everyone waited, a glass in hand, as Harry made a little speech proposing a toast to Martha and the Family.

With their children domiciled in New Zealand, Spain, France, the USA, and Scotland, it was only natural that conversations focused on their experiences living abroad, education, employment and Christmas celebrations. In accents culturally rich, the exchanges covered all the mundane everyday things that shape people's lives in any country on earth. Harry and Martha listening and engaging in the discussions made space for their sons and daughters-in-law to share their stories. If there was a lull in the conversation, Harry, a born storyteller, would tell a story with conviction that would command belief. Martha, on the other hand, was more reticent. She would quietly reflect on her children's adventures and misadventures that coloured their growing up. She would smile shyly, prefacing her reminiscences with, 'Do you remember the day? – Do you remember the time? – Do you remember your father trying to teach you to drive?"

They were happy memories. But their children were adults now, flown the nest with families of their own. Still, Martha ritualistically telephoned every weekend, never missing an anniversary or a birthday, fighting against the natural order to let go. The umbilical cords of motherhood, severely stretched, were not severed. Harry listening to Martha, realised for the first time that she had had a more comprehensive, detailed, intimate relationship with their children than he had. Hence she had a more extensive, more diverse library of memories than his. *Where was I? What was I doing?* He thought. It makes sense, he conceded; after all, she'd spent more time with them. With Christmas night blending seamlessly into Saint Stephen's Day, sleep beckoned all. The house rested.

Parents hoping for a long lie-in on Boxing Day were not spared the attention of their offspring. Informality, the order of the day, fostered a self-catering modus operandi. Martha and Harry withdrew into the background. Saint Stephen's day began the ritual of visitation. Their children spent the day catching up with relations and friends. It was a ritual that would continue until they would leave to journey back home. Florence, on her visits, had eyes for gardens and parks. The majestic trees in the town's nearby parks, Drumalis and Carnfunnock, she found irresistible and must-see places to revisit.

Martha and Harry had the house to themselves. A quiet calm settled around them. Thankful for the gift of family, in their hearts of hearts, they knew that post-Boxing Day, preparations for their departures would begin – all too soon. It was something they would endure with discretion.

In the evening, the house buzzed with energy again. There was much to share. The craic was good. But the conversation soon focussed on the family treat arranged for Friday, which was the afternoon performance of '*Beauty and the Beast*' in the Opera House in Belfast. Everyone was looking forward to it.

On Friday morning, the children carried on doing what children do. As noon approached, a trickle of excitement meandered through the house. By lunchtime, the trickle was a stream. Excitement saturated the air, feverish, tasteable. Chatter among the children was all about the seating arrangements in the theatre. Who would sit beside whom? Parents concerned about behaviour or, more correctly misbehaviour, settled matters. On time the minibus arrived, and everyone scrambled on board. The stream of excitement was now a torrent.

Martha and Harry had made the forty-five-minute journey to the opera house many times. This time it was different. Their group numbered twenty-five, including thirteen excited, boisterous children. On Thursday evening, Harry had gathered them in front of a big fire in the dimly lit family room and proceeded to whet their appetites for the visit to the theatre. By way of a bedtime story, on reflection, not a good idea, he told them about the 'Beauty And The Beast'. He embellished, exaggerated and fantasized with good intent, as he always did when telling a story. Belle, Harry told them, a beautiful young girl, lived with her father. She dreamt of a better life. Her father searching for happiness for her, lost his way on a journey. Bad people sent him to the wrong place, and he found himself outside a big house, surrounded by the most beautiful roses he had ever seen. He picked a rose to take home to his beautiful daughter Belle. But he was captured by an evil beast and imprisoned in the big house. He didn't return home when he said he would. Belle, worried, went to look for him, but she too was taken prisoner by the evil beast.

Inside the big house, Belle discovered that it was full of magical characters. And guess what?"

That's when Harry, teasing, said, "It's getting late, time for beddy bye-byes. We have a big day tomorrow, don't we?"

The children bombarded him with pleas for more.

"Tell us what happened?" As one they urged.

Harry challenged their imaginations. "Tell you what," he said, "why don't we have a competition. How do you think the pantomime will end? There'll be a prize for the best answer," Harry added encouragingly.

On the journey to the opera house, the children's imaginations soared.

The opera house was a hive of activity. Squeezing their way through jostling patrons, they entered a foyer crammed with adults and excited children; anticipation filled the vast volume. A loud bell sounded, the foyer hushed, and the theatre doors opened. Resisting the urge to stampede, they made their way as a group, slowly to row E, five rows back from the orchestra pit. Eventually everyone was seated as prearranged. The auditorium of the opera house looked its magnificent best. The elevated ornately decorated boxes and carved fronted balconies wrapped around the theatre formed an enclosure topped with a ceiling of framed painted panels heightening expectations. Coralie, Frank's wife, was impressed.

The clamorous auditorium hushed expectantly as the lights dimmed, the opening bars of music sounded, and the curtain slowly opened, revealing the set. At that moment, – *the gathering* was reduced to twenty-five spellbound children, among a theatre full of children of all ages. Perched on the edges of their seats, the magic of pantomime transported them into the realms of fantasy.

All too soon, the final curtain closed to thunderous applause. In the minibus back home, the chatter among the children was about the ending of the story. Whose was closest to the finale in the opera house? Around the supper table, 'Beauty and the Beast' was naturally the topic of conversation. The production, the sets, the lighting, the special effects and the music all attracted comment. But especially the happy ending! The children's imaginations hadn't quite soared high enough, but Martha made sure each child got a prize – *all twenty-five of them.*

On Saturday, Harry and Martha had the house to themselves again. Their family was out on their final round of courtesy visits. The mood was sombre. Martha busied herself baking cakes. He could taste the sadness mushrooming in her. Harry withdrew into himself. Their woe filled the room. The walls absorbed it. Their daughter and her family would be the first to leave. They always celebrated the New Year in Edinburgh. Their imminent departure fostered mixed emotions. They didn't discuss it. Didn't need to; Harry and Martha knew they would leave. They had to. Pottering about Harry recalled from vaults of memory words of Tennyson:

'Ring out the old, ring in the new,
Ring, happy bells, across the snow:
The year is going, let him go:
Ring out the false, ring in the new.

Ring out the grief that saps the mind,
For those that here we see no more:
Ring out the feud of rich and poor,
Ring in redress to all mankind. '

Harry mused; *every day's a new beginning. One step at a time. We've got to make the best of it. They have to go and find light for themselves to grow.*

Thanks be to God, they've come into their own. We've nothing to worry about.

Their family filtered home in the early evening. Harry and Martha, innermost feelings concealed, busied themselves helping with the evening meal. It was a relaxed buffet, and thoughts were threshed and sieved, extracting the richness of another day. The quiet man, Owen, found his distinctive, resonant voice to regale *the gathering* with funny stories about aspects of his work that clients misunderstood. Others added flavours of their own.

Suddenly, abruptly, it seemed, the weekend disappeared like swallows at the end of summer. On Sunday evening, their daughter Deidre and family made ready to travel back to Scotland on the early morning ferry. After seeing in the New Year with Martha and Harry, the others would depart for New Zealand, Spain, France, and the United States of America. The ache of parting lay like acid in the bellies of Martha and Harry, and there was no relief from their heartburn.

As things turned out, they could have much to look forward to. Pondering on what they might do in the year ahead, a suggestion surfaced; that they visit their families abroad. The idea, enthusiastically tossed around, gained traction. For Harry and Martha, the future began to look very promising.

Early on Monday morning, Harry and Martha waved goodbye to Deidre and her family on board the ferry bound for Scotland.

The New Year's Eve supper celebration was traditional and straightforward. A roasted joint of bacon with colcannon. Martha served the colcannon elements separately: champ, shredded boiled cabbage, pan finished in the bacon joint juices and sautéed baby leeks. Michael's New Zealand wife Denise, wondered why an empty chair was at the table.

"The empty chair calls to mind those not with us," Harry explained and carried on talking about other customs and traditions.

"I always put a few pounds in Martha's purse to make sure she has a prosperous year ahead, and why do you think we were busy tidying up the house? Sure don't you always want to start the New Year with a clean slate? Here's another one," Harry in full flow continued, "at midnight tonight, we'll open the front door to let the old year out and the New Year in. What do you do in New Zealand on New 'Year's Eve Denise?" Harry enquired.

"We go to the beach, have a barbecue and party. It's summer with us, don't forget," she responded, laughing. "It will be a different experience if you spend Christmas and New Year with us," she continued.

The thought resonating with Harry lingered. Around the table, New Year cultural traditions and anecdotes were eagerly exchanged. Martha went about her business making room on the table for dessert, homemade plum and rhubarb tarts, which she served with generous helpings of almond flavoured ice cream.

It was close to midnight when supper finished; they waited for the tall clock to strike the hour as the ships in the harbour sounded their horns. On the transition hour, they touched glasses in salutation and drank in celebration. Harry rose, took the floor and to the tune of 'The Dawning of the Day' sang an ancient blessing:

"May your nets be always very full,
Your pockets never empty.
May your good horse not need a shoe,
Nor the devil look at you.
May the coming year,
Bring your good cheer,

18

In all, you have to say,
For its a long, long way
From the start of the new
To the ending of it too."

Florence and Coralie encouraged Gabriela to unearth her violin and strike a chord or two. It was that sort of celebration. Those with party pieces sang songs, recited poems, or told stories. The children, those still awake, joined in too. The festivities continued long into the early morning of the New Year.

They slept unaware of happenings in China.

The morning was bright and brisk, tempting Harry and Martha to take a long slow invigorating walk. Dreading the departures to come, they busied themselves preparing breakfast, concealing their anguish.

By Sunday 5th January 2020, Martha and Harry were alone. Their family had departed, dispersed. They had time to themselves, to be with each other, reflecting on – *the gathering* – what more they could have done and perhaps have done better. It was a long reflection, filled with happy memories, inevitably etched with the pain of separation.

Harry reminded Martha that when the Magi visited the Christ child, they left to go home too. That thought filled their emptiness with hope, as did the possibility of reunions in the year ahead. They discussed the pros and cons, what would be involved, would they be fit to cope with travelling long distances and all the stuff that occupies the mind of folk their age going abroad. In the end, they decided to go for it.

Harry enthusiastically immersed himself in the task of making travel plans. Should they travel west to east or east to west? All sorts of computations and considerations occupied his thinking and conversations with Martha. Harry eagerly beavered away on their 2020 travel itinerary, oblivious of a mysterious outbreak of pneumonia in China.

He didn't know that a tsunami of a virulent disease flooding the world would soon drown his plans.

He was about to find out.

Is It Fake News

Bells rang out loudly in celebration across the United Kingdom, announcing the arrival of 2020. Carefree, boisterous crowds gathered in city centres. There was much merrymaking. It was party time. Fireworks illuminated cityscapes.

Early in December 2019, a UK student in Wuhan, China became ill, was hospitalised, recovered, and discharged. Later in December 2019, a cluster of cases of pneumonia in Wuhan Hubei Province was reported, and a new SARS2, coronavirus, COVID-19, was identified. The World Health Organisation informed the world about a cluster of cases in Wuhan in January 2020. COVID-19 was confirmed in Thailand in mid-January, with suggestions of human-to-human transmission. With no reported cases of COVID-19 in the UK, events in China and Thailand were of little concern and media coverage was sparse.

Harry and Martha busied themselves, finalising their travel plans and events in China were of no concern. But by the end of January, there were nearly 8000 confirmed cases of COVID-19 worldwide, with 82 being reported across 18 countries outside China. The virus was on the move, rapidly spreading. The UK warned citizens not to travel to China. Russia closed its borders with China. Italy declared a state of emergency and British

Airways cancelled flights to China. Martha and Harry, different destinations in mind, weren't worried. The spread of the virus didn't concern them – yet. China was a faraway place and they weren't planning to go anywhere near it.

Two cases of COVID-19 were identified in the UK on January 31st; a third was confirmed on February 6th, followed by another on February 27th. A person arriving at Dublin airport from Italy travelled north by bus to Belfast, bringing the virus onto the island of Ireland. By the end of February, the trickle of confirmed cases in the UK had become a stream, and the first wave had arrived on British and Irish shores.

Harry and Martha perceiving no imminent threat, carried on about their business as usual, in their bubble. With family living in different parts of the world Harry realised that what was news in one country was often seldom mentioned in another. But the media sensed a story, and Harry noticed that the number of confirmed cases of COVID-19 had rapidly increased. Still, he wasn't too bothered.

"There's lots of fake news floating about these days, can't be too careful," he said, assuaging Martha's concern.

Harry had nearly finalised their plans for visiting family overseas; he had only a few loose ends to tidy up before booking their trip of a lifetime.

In mid-February, continuing their weekend video conferencing routine, their first port of call was to Michael and family in New Zealand. On this occasion, the content and tone of the video conference with his son forced Harry to think differently. In language that he would not ordinarily use, Michael made it crystal clear to his father just how serious the situation worldwide had become.

"The Australian and New Zealand governments are very concerned about the rapid spread of the virus! They don't want to let it into their countries. This virus is serious stuff, Dad, and" he continued, "they're talking about closing the borders. Australia and New Zealand closing their borders! Can you believe it? This outbreak is worse than the Spanish flu, and it spreads like wildfire. The UK should close its borders now! Take it seriously; your lives are at serious risk. Do you not understand that this thing is deadly?"

"But…but, what about our plans to visit you all?" Harry spluttered,

"You don't get it, Dad. Are you serious? Forget the visits; they're out of the question. Have you booked anything?"

"Well, we were going to book on Monday,"

"Don't! Do you hear me, Dad? Don't! From now on you and Mum need to be very careful, people everywhere, especially those your age, are at high risk! The virus is very easily transmitted, and it's airborne. Remember what Mum used to tell us when we were kids? *Coughs and sneezes spread diseases.* Dad, you better believe it! This is for real."

Michael, as he spoke, was becoming more and more animated. He was almost ranting. Martha intervened, deflecting Michael, asking about his family. The conversation lightened, the tone changed, but not for long. Michael, back onto COVID-19, outlined all the precautions they were taking and what their children had to do in school.

"Everyone in New Zealand is on COVID-19 red-alert, Mum! Don't let dad book your trip, please," he pleaded.

Exchanges continued with the grandchildren and Denise, Michael's wife. Michael very calmly signing off, deliberately stressed again the threat the virus posed to everyone worldwide.

Harry's family in Spain, France, and the United States dispelled his lingering doubts when they vigorously reiterated what Michael had spelt out. Harry and Martha got the message, but they couldn't conceal their disappointment. Expressions like, *you know it's for the best*, at the time didn't cut it for them; their expectations had soared sky-high. With the bottom ripped out of their plans, their descent down to earth was slow and painful. Deidre offered a ray of sunshine, suggesting they spend Christmas and New Year with her in Edinburgh.

At the beginning of March, there were 36 confirmed cases of COVID-19 in the UK, and experts suggested the widespread transmission of the virus was 'highly likely'. Just two weeks later, the number of confirmed cases of COVID-19 in the UK reached 600, and the level of risk was considered high. The UK government published an action plan to deal with Covid-19 that included a scenario for a *severe prolonged pandemic as experienced in 1918*. The Spanish Flu pandemic in 1918 killed 50 million people worldwide. Local government elections were postponed for twelve months, citizens with continuous coughs or fever were advised to self–isolate for seven days, with schools recommended to cancel trips abroad.

The number of confirmed cases of Covis-19 in the UK continued to rise. Stock markets faltered, the value of the pound dropped. Football matches, music festivals and similar events were cancelled. The Prime Minister advised everyone against any non-essential travel and contact with others. He encouraged people to avoid visits to pubs, clubs, theatres, and, if possible, to work from home.

'I do think, looking at it all, that we can turn the tide within the next twelve weeks, and I am absolutely confident that we can send the coronavirus packing in this country, but only if we take the steps, we all take the steps we have outlined,' the Prime Minister said in mid-March.

The next day the government announced the closure of public venues. The Chancellor of the Exchequer introduced a furlough scheme for workers. Later it emerged that the Prime Minister's senior advisor had driven hundreds of miles to self-isolate with COVID-19 symptoms. Then the Health Secretary had to self-isolate. The Prime Minister, having contracted Covid-19, was hospitalised.

The Queen addressed the Commonwealth on television, asking people to 'take comfort that while we have more to endure, better days will return. We will be with our friends again.'

"It's getting serious now, Harry, when the Queen is on the television reaching out to everyone," Martha muttered,

"Well, at least the Queen is believable,"

"What do you mean?"

"You can't believe what other people are saying,"

"You can't believe the Prime Minister?"

"How could you believe anybody with hair like that?"

"It was probably windy that day."

"Must have been blowing a bloody gale."

"You're so harsh."

"You're always making excuses for them."

"He can't help it, can he?"

"Of course, he can. You don't understand. It's deliberate. It's a tool. It's a cultivated persona, an image – windblown, easygoing, approachable, carefree, fun-loving, cuddly etcetera. "

"Don't be silly."

"I'm not. I think it says, 'I'm careless, I don't give a dam, I can't be bothered combing my hair, I'm all about self'"

"He's not like that."

"He's conned you. You think he's cuddly, needs mothering, don't you?"

"Don't be ridiculous. You're starting to annoy me."

"Look what he's wearing. He's dressed for the part."

"What are you on about now?"

"His suit, he's a clown."

"What's wrong with it."

"What's wrong with it? You'd get better suits in the charity shops down the town."

"OK, Harry, that's enough."

"Fine, but the people at the top of Government, making all the rules and giving advice, are the ones getting COVID-19. They're not heeding their own advice. What are they playing at? Do they know what they're doing? Are they fit for purpose?"

"Never thought of that right enough."

"Think about this. The PM's senior advisor in Downing Street can't get childcare in London and drives hundreds of miles to find it. What sort of government can't provide childcare, in an emergency, for a senior colleague? If it can't do something like that, what confidence can we have in their handling of the pandemic?"

"I don't know Harry."

"Neither do I, Martha."

It was happening so quickly that they could hardly believe it.

"Just as Michael said," Harry remarked to Martha, "it spreads like wildfire."

Adjusting to the new normal, they settled into a routine of early morning walks, weekend WhatsApp family video conferences and busying themselves with bits and bobs around the house. Their seasonal group activities had finished before the imposition of lockdown. Gradually they changed their mode of shopping, preferring the safer click and collect options. The thing that most impacted them was the closure of the leisure centre. They loved swimming. Three times a week, they were in the pool early in the morning doing their lengths. Swimming eased Martha's arthritis.

With Easter approaching, preceded by the sombre season of Lent, the UK COVID-19 attributed deaths were more than 9000, and total deaths recorded were significantly higher than seasonal averages. Martha and Harry opted not to attend the Easter liturgies in church for the first time in decades of married life; they chose to participate remotely.

"Better be safe than sorry; stay out of crowds. It's only common sense," Harry persuaded Martha.

The government announced immediately after Easter that lockdown restrictions would continue for at least another three weeks. By the end of April, deaths in the UK attributed to COVID-19, including deaths in care homes, were almost 30,000.

Lockdown for Harry and Martha was an inconvenience. The most annoying thing for Harry was having to book a tee time at the golf club. An early riser, he wanted to be out early to play the back nine on his own. He didn't bother anybody. A free spirit, he wanted to play when he felt like it, as he had always done. He would be out on the course in summer as the sun was rising, play nine holes and be back home for breakfast with Martha, and the rest of the day would be his to do with whatever he and Martha wanted. He found the whole business of booking a tee time tedious; he felt he was losing his freedom. It was an annoyance he could do without, even though he understood the reason for it.

COVID-19 deaths had increased again when the Prime Minister told the UK it was, *'past the peak of this disease'*.

"Can you believe him, Martha?" virus wary Harry asked Martha, extracting an, 'I don't think so' in response.

Vigilantly they continued their daily routines. They weren't shielding but were becoming charier and increasingly careful. It was too risky to visit friends in care homes. They kept in touch by phone and left little gifts. It was their way of saying we haven't forgotten you.

With the lengthening days, spring bulbs brightened their garden. Harry and Martha noticed a worrying tendency creeping into people's behaviour on their early morning and evening walks. It was casual, bordering on a careless disregard for social distancing. Deference behaviour, notwithstanding social distancing, was something from another era. Young people and dog walkers, in particular, showed little consideration for others sharing the pavement.

"They think it's all over," Harry said to Martha, stepping off the pavement into the road, making way for a dog pulling its walker along.

"I know. People should know better. They seem to have little consideration for anybody." Martha muttered.

"It's a societal disease. Individualism and relativism have been around a long time."

"Didn't the World Health Organisation say it's a pandemic?"

"I know and you know, but how many people are listening?"

"Especially the young ones, they think they are indestructible."

"That's what they've been led to believe, but didn't we all, at their age, Martha."

"It was a different world then."

"Well, that's as may be, one thing for sure, quick decisive action, is needed to contain a Pandemic."

"No wonder the Australians and New Zealanders closed their borders."

"No wonder is right; that's what we should have done."

COVID-19 deaths in the UK were the highest in Europe when the government eased lockdown restrictions in May.

"I don't get it, Martha; what is going on?"

Martha's shrug spoke volumes.

It wasn't over, far from it. Also in May, a Covid-19 crisis in care homes surfaced, confirmed infections in the UK continued their upward trajectory and arrivals on international flights into the UK were required to quarantine. COVID-19 deaths exceeded 40,000. Restrictions in the UK continued through the summer months, with local lockdowns imposed where and when deemed necessary. The government introduced public briefings to inform the public of measures to protect the national health service (NHS). The wearing of face coverings indoors in shops and public places was made compulsory.

"Sure, it was only a while ago they were telling us that wearing face masks was a waste of time, Harry?"

"I know. What is the government playing at?"

"Are they making this up as they go along, or what?"

"Sometimes it's hard to know who or what to believe."

"It can't be fake news? Can it? It's our government."

"No, it's politics getting in the way of common sense."

"Do you remember when we were in Beijing, everybody wore masks?" Martha said recalling a long-ago holiday.

"Aye and with good reason, and it's going to be the same here."

"Do you think so?"

"It's a regulation now, but the habit will catch on. Mark my words."

"Think so?"

"It's like seat belts and smoking. Government can make it work if it wants to."

"Sign of the times then. Are we heading for another lockdown, do you think?"

"I'm sure of it. Know why? People have little sense. Just look around you. I think we can cancel Christmas in Edinburgh, the way things are going."

"You're not serious?"

"I'm deadly serious, Martha."

They found the Government's televised news briefings confusing and depressing. They switched off and got on with their lives. They didn't have to shield, nor worry about employment, they had a garden to enjoy, were blessed with good health and had the freedom to exercise unhindered. They had concerns about their family—especially their family in Spain. Containment measures there were more severe than in the UK. Assurances that everyone was okay didn't assuage their concerns. Harry, ever the pragmatist, knew there was little they could do to help, but it was a thought he concealed from Martha.

Restrictions eased, allowing gyms, swimming pools and leisure centres to reopen. Martha and Harry thought it was just too risky to go swimming again. An – *eat out to help out* scheme, in support of the hospitality sector, was introduced to which many eagerly lent their support. Harry and Martha didn't participate; they weren't dropping their guard.

With autumn approaching, the number of confirmed Covid-19 cases in the UK rapidly increased. The Prime Minister spoke of a perilous turning point being reached. New social distancing measures were introduced, and mass virus testing gained momentum. Media reports indicated that cases of COVID-19 in the UK might reach 50,000 per day unless the government intervened. Experts feared a second wave was imminent, and the government urged people to rethink their plans for Christmas.

When another lockdown was announced in November, Martha and Harry cancelled Christmas in Edinburgh because they thought it too risky. Harry had binned their travel insurance renewal notice long ago and with it their dreams for 2020. In hope, he filed their itinerary for future use – possibly 2021. Now, even Edinburgh, a stone's throw away, was beyond reach.

Lockdown reintroduced, Christmas in Edinburgh ruled out, Harry and Martha prepared to celebrate Christmas at home; their roast turkey expectations downsized to roast chicken. It would be a quiet affair—Martha and Harry's Christmas barbecue on a New Zealand beach, now a distant pipe dream.

"It's a long way from last Christmas to this one," Martha remarked.

"Feels like it right enough, dear."

"And folk often say there's no distance between the one and other."

"It's not the distance Martha; it's what happens in between that makes your days shorter or longer. Remember the song we used to sing years ago? 'The best of all ways to lengthen your days is to steal a few hours from the night, my dear', do you remember? Didn't we steal a few hours, Martha?'

"I mind all right, 'The Young May Moon'. How could I forget it?

With winter days shortening rapidly and nights lengthening, the garden became less hospitable. Inclement weather curtailed their walks. The drama club cancelled its programme of activities. The Folklore Club and the Choral Society followed suit. Suddenly all the activities they looked forward to were unavailable. Television offered nothing more than a succession of repeated repeats. Their silent church provided little solace. Fortunately, they found spiritual consolation online. It was after availing of various online services, Harry remarked, "I think our priests are going to have to pull their socks up."

"I think so too."

"Will it ever be the same again?"

"We'll probably carry on as before; the church is slow to change."

"Young people wouldn't hang around waiting for change. They look for inspirational leadership."

"Changed times indeed."

"The evidence is out there. Young ones won't hang around waiting."

"What do you mean?"

"There's so much going on in young people's lives, Martha. They carry libraries of information around in their hands. Smart phones and all sorts of devices are everyday tools to them – not like us – afraid of them- unable to keep up. Group chat, peer relationships, social media are very important to them too. We had none of that in our day. Had we? If we can't cope, we opt out, step aside and let it pass us by if we can. It's not so easy for the young ones."

"It's too much for me, Harry. The way you put it, I feel sorry for them."

For the first time, they felt alone, isolated. Cut off. Harry lost interest in the garden. The fallen leaves lay wet and matted on the lawn. Wilted flowers he would have replaced with bedding plants lay in sodden disarray. Martha, despite her arthritis, started to rake the lawn, hoping that she might kick-start Harry into action. Harry sat in his favourite chair, disinterestedly watching her through the window, labouring. Eventually, he re-alised she wasn't labouring. Martha wasn't moving. She was im-mobile, hunched over, leaning on the rake, with both hands looking as if she was about to collapse. The thought of her fall-ing onto the ground and hurting herself roused Harry from his apathetic torpidity. Rushing to her, he put his head on her chest, buttressed himself against her, eased the rake away, let it fall to the ground, and with his arms wrapped around her, held Martha close.

"In the name of all that's holy, what happened, Martha?"

"I don't know. I just froze, Couldn't move."

"Are you ok now?"

"I think so, a bit dizzy."

"Can you walk?"

"I'll try, hold onto to me."

"Ok, let's go to the bench over there and sit down. We'll take it easy."

"That's better; I don't know what came over me."

"Did you have breakfast?"

"I don't remember."

"Did you take your medication?"

"Stop it, Harry. Stop interrogating me."

"I didn't mean to. I'm worried about you, that's all."

"Do you think I wasn't worried about you, sitting there looking out at nothing day after day."

"I... I... I'm sorry."

"I had to get out and do something otherwise..."

"It's my fault, I'm sorry."

"No! It's not. I just did too much. Sometimes things overwhelm us until we realise that's it not all sunshine, some days our skies are overcast."

"Let's go in. I'll put the kettle on."

They sat a little while in silence before leaving the garden.

After tea, as Martha rested, Harry finished the job she'd started in the garden, raking and binning the windfall from the cotoneasters. The cloud that had darkened his mind lightened and drifted away. Inwardly he acknowledged that he had, in his head, to convert the reality of the pandemic into something positive. It was simple. Care for each other's well-being. Why hadn't he thought of it before? All they had to do was identify things they enjoyed doing together and embrace the opportunities. Harry had found himself again.

Every evening through autumn and winter, except Saturdays and Sundays, they had been involved in some activity or other. That was something that had never occurred to them before. They had taken it all for granted. It only surfaced when they sat down to consider what to do with their free evenings, courtesy of COVID-19. They had books to read and some to reread. Reading was pencilled in for two evenings. Harry liked things calendared. They considered rereading plays they liked, but it felt like overdoing the reading. Martha suggested trying to write something instead. Harry was hesitant.

"It would be fun. Something different! You remember that book. Oh, what was it called? Deidre gave it to us for Christmas."

Harry chewed thoughtfully on his pipe.

"I know," Martha exclaimed, *"The Five Minute Writer.* You know it, Harry, come on, it was full of little exercises in creative writing. It would be great fun. We could have a competition. I bet I could beat you!"

Harry's hook baited; he couldn't resist the challenge. They pencilled creative writing into their weekly calendar. Then Harry had a brainwave.

"Martha, why don't we have a wee prize for the best story each week?"

"It's a great idea, Harry, but I want none of your nonsense now, we're past all that," she laughed.

"Nothing like that dear," Harry said with a laugh. "I was thinking, you know the way in the drama club they video short pieces and post them on the club's Facebook page. We could do that. We could record a reading of what we think is the best piece we write each week and post it on the Club's Facebook page. What do you think?"

Martha wasn't keen, but after some persuading, she agreed. Their weekly calendar of home-based activities, far from complete, consisted only of reading and writing.

"What else can we do of an evening?" Martha asked.

"Puzzles," Harry suggested.

"Sure, we do the crosswords on Sunday afternoons. Think of something new, something different,"

"What like?"

"I don't know. You're the one with the imagination."

"What would you like to do?"

"Something different."

They tossed around lots of ideas before settling on another three to fill their calendar. Photography, with a twist, would add interest to their daily walks. The challenge would be only to photograph the quirky or incongruous, improving their photographic skills while creating a collection of weird and beautiful images. International travel was out of the question for the foreseeable future. They loved Italy and intended to holiday there again. With that hope and their love of opera, they enrolled on a free online Italian language course. In addition, they would unearth all photographs taken, videos recorded, and notes made on holiday in Italy and compile a memoir for posterity.

One of their passions was the game of bridge, but rather than play bridge via zoom; they thought it better to teach themselves to play chess and play against each other competitively once they had mastered the basics. Harry produced a schedule and fixed it with a magnet to the fridge door to remind them what was on each evening. Their activities weren't set in stone, but a routine quickly set.

The time hurtled towards Christmas. They had become co-cooned, self-contained. Their daily walks were either early morning or late evening to avoid people. Their window into the world was 'WhatsApp' video conferences with their family. From, Michael they learned that New Zealand had only forty confirmed COVID-19 cases in October and that the majority of those, despite stringent border controls, were imported. The situation in Spain was grim, and severe containment measures were in place. The increase in confirmed COVID-19 cases in the USA was ringing alarm bells, but President Trump wasn't hearing them. Harry figured he was in denial. Their children's message was – 'look after yourselves' – because it will get much worse in the UK.

With Christmas 2020 just around the corner, Harry and Martha spent a day and an evening looking at photographs and video recordings of Christmas 2019.

"Will we all ever be together again, Harry?"

"Hard to tell, but there's always hope."

"I hope so. It was lovely having them all here."

"They grow up so fast."

"Where does the time go?"

"I don't know! Next time we see our grandchildren, some of them could be at college."

"I don't think they'll ever be back here again, though."

"If the virus can be contained, who knows, maybe we can resurrect our travel plans and go see them."

"You think so?"

"Keep looking forward, Martha. It's the only way."

On the Eve of Christmas night 2020, their dining room table was not as it was for the last Eve of Christmas supper. Two chairs sit side by side at the table facing a blank wall. Lit candles, set in window recesses, flicker flames of love to family abroad and Martha sits waiting for Harry to dim the lights. Joining her, he opens his laptop. This evening they are going to enjoy the videos of last Christmas when they were all together. That's what Martha is expecting! As the tall clock strikes the hour, Harry clicks on the link on his laptop enabling Zoom.

A rectangular array appears on the laptop screen. Five boxes, one for each family, and Martha thinks she is viewing videos of Christmas past for a brief moment! Then she realises that her family is waving and talking to her. Martha can see and speak to them, and it's not a recorded video – it's real time, live streaming. Momentarily stunned, Martha is speechless. Suddenly everyone is talking at once.

Head down, mouth open, staring into the laptop screen, Martha is unaware that what she is seeing is projected onto the blank wall of the dining room in front of her. Raising her head, she sees her extended family, life-size, filling the wall. It is as if they were there with her, and she can almost reach out and touch them. Gasping in disbelief, feelings of joy, gratitude and relief, surge through her like a rampant river in full flood. It takes more than a moment or two for Martha to regain composure. The three hours available on Zoom seem to pass in seconds. Expressions of mutual love are shared with concerns, hopes and aspirations exchanged. Grandchildren too, feature prominently, joining in the chaos of a jubilant, remote, worldwide family Christmas reunion heightened by separation.

Reluctantly they parted with goodbyes tearfully expressed. The New Zealanders enjoyed their beach barbecue, COVID-19 free, Barcelona and Paris were in lockdown, New York was rejoicing over the presidential election result in the middle of a pandemic, and the UK was in COVID-19 disarray. But all that mattered to Martha and Harry was that their family was united, safe and secure.

Pondering over everything that had happened, Martha asked, "Explain to me, Harry, how all that worked?"

"What worked?"

"The pictures on the wall, what do you think!"

"It's just like the TV."

"Did you do all that?"

"No, I got someone to set it up for us."

"Did it cost much?" Martha wanted to know.

"It did. It's the most expensive Christmas present I've given you, Martha."

"You did all that for me, Harry?"

"Sure. Don't you deserve it?"

They sat for a while, nightcaps in hand, mulling over the evening.

Harry broke the silence saying, "You know, I think for us tonight, the world just got a lot smaller. Don't you think?"

"I'd put it another way. They're not as far away as I thought," Martha answered.

Harry sensed her anxieties melting away, knowing they would return. Martha couldn't help it, and that was her nature. The year that was almost gone had not been all plain sailing. They'd had their stressful moments, trouble sleeping, mood changes, bouts of loneliness, and social isolation, but they coped, thinking differently, staying active, and staying positive. It was an attitude they would carry forward into the New Year. Harry's thought's drifted back to the last two verses of Tennyson's poem From In Memoriam:

'Ring out the old shapes of foul disease;
Ring out the narrowing lust of gold;
Ring out the thousand wars of old,
Ring in the thousand years of peace.

Ring in the valiant man and free,
The larger heart, the kindlier hand;
Ring out the darkness of the land,
Ring in the Christ that is to be.'

Christmas day was dawning when they went to bed.

Around the world, nations waited, dreading another COVID wave, perhaps a tsunami. Infections were rapidly increasing. The Prime Minister had warned that the road ahead would be bumpy.

They had hard-boiled eggs and toast for breakfast on Christmas morning. The house was quiet. No church bells sounded. It seemed as if the whole world was anxiously waiting!

"It wasn't this quiet last Christmas morning," Martha pensively remarked.

"No, it wasn't. There was quite a racket."

"They had a great time, though. Didn't they?"

"Of course they had," Harry reassured her.

The noise of excited children last Christmas morning Harry knew was echoing around in Martha's head. She felt for them, as the world it seemed plunged headlong into darkness. They needed a change of scene, something to lift their spirits.

In the sitting room, he searched and found on the internet a recording of the Nativity of the Lord's Mass celebrated in Singapore. It was the Dawn Mass. As they would do in church, they participated, making the responses and listening attentively to the readings. The celebrant for his homily chose the text, 'The people who have walked in darkness have seen a great light.' When the Mass ended, Martha looked at Harry a question in her eyes, "What did you think of that?"

"Uplifting, inspiring."

"What do you mean?

"It's pertinent, relevant."

"For us today?"

"Yes, totally."

"I don't get it."

"It's about God's relationship with his people."

"Sorry, my mind must have been somewhere else."

"The Assyrians invaded Israel, their lands and captives were taken. Ok? The lord then enabled Israel to free itself. They rejoiced because the Lord had rescued them. In the gospel, Jesus, God's Gift, is the light of salvation coming into our world. God rescues his people again. It is a message of hope."

"That's what we need now, alright, hope."

As the New Year approached, Martha's became edgier. She wanted to be with her family. Not content that they were content, she worried about them, and Harry's reassurances did little to ease her worries.

"They were with us last Christmas, Martha. They're all right. They have parents–in–law too, you know, and we can't have them all to ourselves."

Two days before the New Year, they embarked on a round of 'WhatsApp' video calls. Everybody was fine. Martha was reassured.

But Covid clouds were thickening and gathering around the world. What would the new normal be, they wondered?

What would 2021 hold for them?

Time would tell.

Family Matters

Muted celebrations across the United Kingdom (UK) heralded the dawning of another year, plagued by COVID-19. Harry and Martha, veterans of the annual transience, witnessed the moment and went to bed. The morning television and radio broadcasts led with police breaking up illegal New Year celebration parties.

Martha and Harry couldn't believe it. People, out and about celebrating, with the 'R' number ranging between 1.1 and 1.5 and the threat of a significantly more virulent new COVID-19 strain looming. Bemused, they wondered why intelligent people engaged in such juvenile, revelling behaviour in the middle of a pandemic. COVID-19 cases were increasing exponentially; did they not know hospital admissions were rapidly growing and that the number of COVID related deaths was surging? Then, to crown it all, it emerged that people in public office were not following government-issued COVID-19 guidance. Mixed messaging was nurturing confusion. But Harry wasn't confused. He realised that it was time to batten down the hatches.

Harry looked at Martha and shook his head in disgust. There was however good news – *hope*. The first Oxford–AstraZeneca vaccine was administered in the UK on January 4th, but to balance the good news, the daily confirmed number of COVID-19 cases stretched towards 50,000.

The New Year had hardly drawn a breath when the UK plunged into another lockdown.

"Is it any wonder?" Harry remarked to Martha, "sure, weren't they asking for it, behaving like that, only fools would do it, don't you think?"

"People are careless; sure, you see it every day no matter where you go?"

"Don't I know it?"

Harry and Martha plodded on, keeping themselves and those around them as safe as they could. Enthusiastically they pursued activities set in motion during the preceding lockdown. Revisiting with photographs and videos places in Italy added value to their Italian language course. Their spoken Italian improved so much that they could converse naturally in Italian. They didn't notice at first. In the kitchen, cooking anything remotely Italian, they used their increasing fluency with confidence. To revisit Venice remained an enduring hope.

Duelling on the chessboard, by an open fire in the evening with a glass of red wine, was a much looked forward to, relaxing pleasure, although being checkmated was sometimes hard to swallow. It was a competitive pursuit that shielded Martha and Harry from the repetitive 24/7 COVID-19 dominated news bulletins and ritualistic government press briefings.

Searching for odd and quirky things to photograph on their walks took them to many new places. Martha and Harry discovered items that added substance to their story writing in addition to album building. On one of their walks through the townlands above the town, they photographed the remains of a small white van, lying half-hidden in a ditch, resting at peace, driver's side up. The entire windscreen was naked – tax disc free. The four baldy tyres stared unashamedly towards them. The rear doors gaping wide open were like the wings of a giant bird riding the thermals. The van was empty, and persons unknown had removed anything of value, including the number plates.

"It doesn't take much to fire the sparking plug of imagination, does it?" Martha idly remarked,

"Could have been an accident."

"Could have been dumped."

"Could be anything you want it to be."

"Okay, let's write a story about an abandoned white van and see whose is better."

"It has to be an old one, like this beyond salvaging, ok?"

"Ok."

As they walked, threads of stories involving old abandoned white vans percolated in their minds, dispelling other thoughts. Martha's remark about the sparking plug of imagination may have been flippant, but the challenge generated was anything but. They spent hours tossing ideas about, getting nowhere, bogged down. Their sparking plugs were misfiring. It took over a week for them to find the thread of a story and another week to begin working on a first draft. There were many redrafts and conversations before they decided which was the better story.

Finally, they gave it a title: *The ditched van in Killyglen*

Rosemary had just turned thirty. Her parents had passed. An only child, she inherited their home. On weekends she would, with friends, go dancing in the village halls of townlands near and far. Often Rosemary wouldn't know where she was until she left the car and entered the dance hall. It was in one of these faraway places that she met John. He was five years older than her, an only child like her whose parents had passed. John was a farmer

without the bearing of a farmer. It was his gentlemanliness that swept Rose-
mary off her feet onto cloud nine. He was in every respect what she unwit-
tingly was looking for—her Prince Charming.

Their courtship was short and sweet. John's veneer of gentlemanliness
held fast. Rosemary couldn't get married soon enough. Friends tried to per-
suade her to wait. Rosemary, head over heels in love, was not for turning.
She must be pregnant, some thought. The wedding was a quiet affair. They
hadn't planned a honeymoon; John suggested they honeymooned when the
workload on the farm eased.

John farmed one hundred acres. His home, now their home, a quaint
cottage, fitted Rosemary's notion of a love nest. With love bursting her heart,
she set about making it their home. Twelve months into the marriage, Rose-
mary miscarried. She was heartbroken. John, his veneer of gentlemanliness
slipping, shrugged it off, remarking, "Sure, can't we have another try?"

When he left her to check on the sheep, Rosemary wondered if she was
just one of his ewes. He never called her Rosemary again. It was always
Rosie this and Rosie that. They did try for a replacement child; John wanted
a boy. All Rosemary wanted was a healthy baby; boy or girl didn't matter.
But their coupling became loveless and dutiful. She felt like a used ewe—
one of his flock.

In the years that followed, their relationship deteriorated. Rosemary felt
like a servant girl, a skivvy.

"Why am I living like this?" she asked herself. "Why am I putting up
with this?"

By this time, they slept in different bedrooms and John's gentlemanliness
was long absent. Rosemary knew that if she mentioned divorce, she would
be on the receiving end of John's violent temper. The last time he raised his
hand to her, she resolved, was the last time. She would desert him, in her
way, in her time. Let him worry about his standing in the community.

John had an old white van he used for odd jobs about the farm and
around the neighbourhood at night. Never anywhere near where police might
be on duty because the van was neither taxed nor insured. When John was

away somewhere, Rosemary drove it up and down the yard to get used to handling it.

On his night out with his cronies in the village, John used the land rover. He wouldn't be back until late. Rosemary would be in bed. He wouldn't look in to say goodnight.

As John drove off in the Landover towards the village, Rosemary, knapsack on her back, slipped their wedding photograph out of its frame, burned it, waited a little while then followed John out the gate in the white van, She headed in the opposite direction to him.

It was a bright, cloudless, starry, frosty night. The lights on the van were not good, and the steering was slack. Rosemary, driving carefully, had plenty of time to catch the ferry to Scotland. Rounding a bend, a rabbit, or perhaps a hare, maybe even a sheep crossed the road in front of her. Reacting, Rosemary jerked the steering wheel to avoid a collision, skidded, lost control and finished up in the roadside ditch. She was lucky, bruised, but no bones broken.

Standing on the road, rucksack on her back, Rosemary could see the town below lit up. She could see the harbour. Her ferry wasn't there; it wasn't due for hours. If she hurried, she could still make it on foot.

She did. With the proceeds from the sale of her home that John had never got his hands on, Rosemary never looked back.

It had taken Martha and Harry over three weeks to fashion a six hundred word short story. Not that they were counting. The exercise had proved more demanding than they imagined, and it had been hard work.

The weeks spent working on the abandoned van story benefitted their reading too. Their approach became more incisive. They searched for meaning, structure, ingenuity and originality. Reading aloud to each other, the more they listened, really listened, to the rhythms in what they were reading, the more their story writing improved. Sitting at the kitchen table, side by side, feeling the other's presence, sharing ideas, they became lost in the togetherness of the moment.

Harry was rediscovering his mislaid love. He was transported back in thought and time, to an old secluded wooden bench, under the overhanging branches of a sycamore tree at the bottom of the Inver Road. It was a favourite resting place after their trek over the Inver Braes. Always quiet, the only noise, the ripple of the river beside them, on its way to the sea. They would sit talking until it was time to dash for the last bus. Martha had to be home on time. 'Happy, innocent days,' he thought. Harry's trouble was, no matter how hard he tried, he couldn't, for the life of him; remember what it was they talked about.

Martha blissfully unaware of Harry's thoughts, scribbling, filled another page with fresh ideas.

Martha was, by nature, a worrier, and Harry had learned over time that there was no cure for it. If Martha had nothing to worry about, that was a worry too. When writing, there was no space in Martha's head for extraneous thoughts. For the two veterans of marriage, it was an ardent time writing, understanding, tolerating, accommodating, and encouraging each other in different, sometimes not always harmonious, ways. They discerned that writing often was a waiting game, taking hours of thought sometimes before lucidity permitted ink to stain the page. They learned ways of bringing characters in their stories to life, adding colour and gravitas. Some stories shared among friends attracted encouraging comments.

On January 5th, the UK was in lockdown again. Restrictions, including school closures, were expected to last until mid-February. But there was good news. More vaccines were coming online. In the fourth week of January, COVID deaths in the UK exceeded 100,000, and some sources suggested the number was closer to 150,000. In early February, concerns regarding the efficacy of vaccines emerged, and the R number was between 1.0 and 1.4. The government issued reassurances, and fake news, it seemed, was rampant. Experts identified new variants of the coronavirus, confirming that it was mutating.

Martha and Harry received their first COVID-19 vaccinations in the last week of January, with their second dose scheduled for mid-April. Harry experienced no side effects, but Martha was not so fortunate. For four days, she suffered severe muscle soreness and dizzy spells. Then she was back on her feet again, raring to go—much to Harry's relief. But even though they had their first jab, they didn't lower their guard.

Suddenly it was the 17th of February, Ash Wednesday. The sombre season of Lent, the period of penitential preparation for Easter, was upon them. The High Court ruled that the UK's Health Secretary had breached his legal obligations. On the 22nd of February, the Prime Minister set out his roadmap for lifting lockdown that included schools reopening in March, non-essential retail opening in April, social distancing relaxations in May, and the lifting of all limits on social distancing in June. It sounded good.

Too good for Harry and Martha. They paid scant attention to the Prime Minister's roadmap. They knew that the virus was everywhere, and the death toll was rapidly increasing. Harry tried to explain again to Martha what exponential meant. Virologists identified variants of COVID-19 – Kent, Brazilian, African and Indian – the virus had mutated, and it was more insidious. The omens were not good; some biblical voices spoke of the end times. For Martha and Harry, their journey through Lent to Easter Day was sustained by hope. There was hope. Other vaccines were coming online, and all adults in the UK were promised vaccination by the end of July.

They continued using the click and collect options for shopping, wore their face masks in public, avoided crowds, religiously observed social distancing and hand washing. People, it seemed, didn't grasp the gravity of the situation. Social distancing was noticeably waning, deference not even a concept. Thinking that people were more careless, more blasé, reinforced their resolve to look after themselves and others.

Martha and Harry carried on with their busy lives. Little did they know, that was their well-being secret, keeping busy. In Lent, there were moments of celebration. They celebrated their fifty-eighth wedding anniversary on March 1st with family via the internet. Another celebration closely followed. Harry celebrated his eighty-second birthday also with the aid of video links on the 28th of March. But Lent held more surprises.

On the evening of Mother's Day, a live-streamed concert performance of La bohème was available online. Martha and Harry loved La bohème. They had tickets for the concert, courtesy of their family. Harry connected his laptop to their big-screen television, added fuel to the open fire, pulled the sofa closer to the TV, readied the red wine and chocolates and waited for the performance to begin. It was Lent – they were naughty – but it was fun.

Martha and Harry settled before their big screen, hand in hand, like a couple of teenagers, lustily singing the arias in Italian. They didn't reach all the high notes, but they didn't need to; they were high on love's nectar. Martha, afterwards feeling remorseful, said,

"It's Lent; you know Harry?"

"I know it is. But it's not a sin to be happy in Lent, is it?"

"It's just…you know…"

"We can be happy penitents, can't we?"

"We could do a bit more, couldn't we?"

"A bit more of what? Everybody could do a bit more. We're in lockdown. We can't save the whole world!"

"You know what I mean."

"I'm not sure I do. We do what we can, but we have to leave something for Jesus to do. Don't we?"

"That's what you always say."

"You forget. Jesus told us to lay our burdens down."

Tempus fugit and Tempus repit! Sometimes life flies past, and other times it's a waiting game. But waiting for what? Beckett says Godot. In lockdown with places of worship closed, it felt like gloom had settled over the world.

In March, a former senior aide to the Prime Minister criticised the Department of Health as being 'a smoking ruin in terms of procurement and personal protection equipment at the start of the pandemic.' The Health Secretary confirmed that reduced vaccine supplies would affect people getting their second doses. The Prime Minister informed the nation that he had received his first jab. Excess mortality in the 65's and over was nearly 8% higher than the average in the winter of 2020-21. More fake news?

Worsening COVID-19 UK conditions in the UK forced the extension of lockdown until April 1st, and there was great uncertainty about what might happen after that. The only remaining ray of hope for Martha and Harry spending the next Christmas with any of their family depended on what was happening in Scotland. Covid-19 related deaths in the UK were surging.

On the Sunday evening after Easter day, Harry put the chess set away, and Martha made the last of her family phone calls. Reaching for the phone, she was surprised when it came to life. Instinctively she pulled her hand away as if stung before circumspectly picking it up. Her weekend chats with the family weren't brief encounters, far from it, yet this phone call was longer than usual. Much longer. When Martha joined Harry, it was plain to see that something was troubling her. She sat beside him. Harry waited, said nothing.

In a nutshell, Agnes, her best friend Moira's youngest child, a college student, had issued her mother an ultimatum. She wasn't going back to school after Easter. As far as Agnes was concerned, there was no point in it. She didn't want to be a slave to the national health service like her mother. Harry said nothing.

Martha, he was thinking, *you wanted a bit more to do. You've got what you wished for.*

Martha and Moira were longstanding friends. When her husband died in a road traffic accident, Martha helped Moira rebuild her life. It wasn't easy. Moira, a senior NHS theatre nurse, had three young daughters to care for, in addition to being the breadwinner. Slowly she gathered up the threads of life again. Denise, her eldest child and her sister Megan, three years her junior, were in their final and first years respectively at university. Agnes, the youngest of the trio, and Harry and Martha's Godchild, was in college, with high expectations of going on to university to study medicine. Lockdown had forced home learning on Moira's daughters.

Working the extra shifts required through the pandemic, Moira assumed that everything at home was as it should be, ordinary, natural. Her girls, she thought, were old enough to look after themselves and each other.

There were times Agnes didn't see much of her mother. But she saw enough and felt deeply the demands work made on her. Agnes, fully aware of her mother's risks at work, noticed how tired she was. Her sisters focused on their studies, didn't seem to notice. With time to brood and no one to talk to, Agnes concluded that for her, it would be pointless to spend years studying medicine to end up like her mother, a slave, working ten-hour shifts week in, week out, like a headless chicken for the NHS.

Moira arrived home on Sunday morning after another night shift, tired as usual. That was the moment; Agnes chose to deliver her ultimatum. Moira, stunned, desperately collecting her thoughts, trying to grasp the import of Agnes's confrontation, suggested it might be better to talk things over after she had a little rest. Agnes, furious, ran from the house, slamming the door shut, leaving her bewildered mother standing alone in the kitchen. Moira, too tired to run after Agnes, sought bed, hoping to rest. She couldn't sleep; her daughter's outburst wriggled in her head.

Harry was digesting what Martha had told him when she said, "Harry, take the car out. Let's go over to Moira's."

Moira ushered them inside. She was wearing dark glasses. In the lounge, unmasked, socially distanced, Moira, without her glasses, looked haggard, tired, and wearied. It was plain to see that she'd been crying. Martha resisted the desire to wrap Moira in a loving hug. They sat in silence for a little while. Composing herself, Moira told them the whole story.

"I was working nights—four nights on, three days off. With the pandemic and shortage of staff, I worked extra shifts. It was tough. At times I crawled into bed when I got home. Denise and Megan are fully occupied with their university courses online. I thought Agnes was likewise engaged online with her 'O' levels. The house was like a student's residence. But each of the girls have a room of their own. Everything seemed ok.

"I'd do the housework, stock up the fridge, keep the house in order, etcetera. Denise and Megan could meet up with university friends studying at home occasionally. I didn't realise Agnes was socially disadvantaged. You know her school is twenty miles away, and she hardly knows anybody her own age here, in

51

her own home town. It was one of those things; everyone thinks everyone else is ok. I never thought, it didn't occur to me; I was so engrossed in the work that I'd forgotten about Agnes."

Fighting back the tears, she carried on.

"It's too easy not to see the concern in a quiet person like Agnes. I was blind.

"I didn't know that Agnes would often go out for hours walking when I was asleep after a night shift. Worse, she was also going out at night when I was working nights and staying out late, very late. God only knows who she could have met. I was unaware of any of this. So were Denise and Megan, but that's no excuse. They knew she went out occasionally for a walk, that's all. She's like most teens, she sleeps a lot."

Moira inclined her head for Harry and Martha to follow her. Tiptoeing, they peeked into Agnes's bedroom. Agnes lay face down on her bed, still in her jeans, sneakers discarded by her bed, one arm hanging by the bedside, her head resting on the other, her fingers curled into her hands. Her breathing was deep and regular. Her freckled face flushed. They retreated quietly back to the lounge. Moira continued her story.

"After Agnes's outburst, I couldn't sleep. I got up around lunchtime, made some tea and toast, and looked into Agnes's room. She wasn't there, wasn't in the house. It was around tea time when she came home. I was getting ready for work. I said something flippant, I suppose, like, 'Hi Agnes, had a good day?' She erupted again, yelling at me as if I was a scoundrel and all hell broke loose. It was all my fault. Denise and Megan left what they were doing and rushed down to see what was going on. Agnes was ranting about not going back to school; it was a waste of time, she'd had enough. I was shocked. Denise and Megan managed to calm her down. I didn't know what to do. I had to go to work. People depended on me. But so did Agnes!"

Martha again wanted to comfort her friend, yet social distancing forbade it. She managed a smile of encouragement. "Go on, Moira, get it all out," she said.

"Denise and Megan convinced me that there was nothing useful to be done until Agnes calmed down. They assured me they would take care of her. I went to work, and I do not know how I got through that shift without mishap, but thank God I did. Agnes slept all day. Denise and Megan discovered that Agnes had missed some online tuition. We talked things over, what best to do, should we seek counselling for her, talk to the school obviously, perhaps she had difficulty coping with her studies. That and much more was ratcheting around in my head. Then I thought of you, needed your shoulders."

She looked weary but not defeated. Shrugging her shoulders, relieving momentarily the anxieties whirling around in her head, Moira slowly got up, walked over to the east-facing bow window, opened wide the Venetian blinds saying, "Time to let some daylight in, don't you think?" Sitting down, she looked at Martha and asked,

"What do you think?"

"She's young, growing up, finding her feet; you know what it's like."

"You think so?"

"It's part of growing up. Finding our way."

"God, I hope so."

"Don't overthink this, creating problems where there may be none, one step at a time. Agnes is a young girl growing up in strange times. Didn't we all have problems growing up in the best of times?"

"Different now though, in our day social media was the local newspaper. It's everywhere now 24/7, smart phones and all. The world of young ones is moving faster than ours did."

"Folk like Harry and me can withdraw from it all and let it pass, but the young can't really. Can they?"

They sat in silence with their thoughts. Harry was aware of Agnes first. She, having ghosted into the room, stood motionless inside the door. She looked sad, helpless, lost. Her unplaited, unkempt hair drooped lifelessly around her shoulders, no light shone in her sunken eyes, her pallid face shrouded its freckles, and her arms dangled at her sides, fingers slowly curling and uncurling. It was as if she was sleepwalking. Agnes jolted awake when Harry stood up, reached out his hand in greeting and spoke in his deep baritone voice, "Agnes, how are you dear? We haven't seen you in a while?"

She clasped her hands over her mouth, covering a flicker of a smile, a smile Harry interpreted as a cry for help. Joining her mother on the settee, they chatted. Colour returned to Agnes's cheeks, and her eyes brightened. Not wanting to overstay their welcome, Martha signalled secretly to Harry that it was time to take their leave as only soul mates can.

At home, Harry and Martha mulled over their evening. Their Godchild was a quiet, shy child who affectionately called them Auntie Martha and Uncle Harry. But she was a tough, wiry little girl, loved sports, took to tennis like a duck to water, was a grade four pianist and expectations had always been that she would follow in her sisters' footsteps to university. Her jaunty, bouncy way of walking always made Harry smile. The loss of her father was harrowing for the family, but they had moved on, it seemed. Now, years later, Agnes, a casualty of COVID-19 imposed lockdowns, was giving vent to deep-seated dormant feelings.

Martha and Harry knew that Moira would like any parent; go to the college, meet the principal, talk with Agnes's form teacher, seek support groups, trawl the internet, spend hours googling, seek guidance from any and every available credible source, and consult their GP. Was it just a coming of age issue? They wondered.

Harry and Martha addressed themselves to what they could best do? Harry suggested that professionals best-handled concerns about the adverse effects of lockdown on young people and that they should assume Agnes was befuddled, disconcerted, and confused.

"We've all been there in adolescence, one way and another, haven't we, Martha?"

"One way and another, yes."

"Well, if Agnes is confused, uncertain about something, or mixed up, maybe she just needs someone to talk to. Someone she can trust. Someone like us, perhaps?"

"You might be right. Can you imagine what it must be like three or four people working from home? Their noses in their work. Can't be easy? Can it?"

Martha's thoughts threaded quickly back to a time when she didn't want to go to school. She didn't see the point. All she saw in front of her was factory work, which didn't much whet her young appetite. The irony was that without a decent education, the factory was her destiny. Working-class parents, busy putting bread on the table for the family, did the best they could but weren't best equipped to advise. Fortunately for Martha, others were. She completed her schooling, avoided factory entrapment and found her vocation in nursing.

"You might be onto something Harry."

"I was wondering, Martha, you know that stuff about long lasting COVID?"

"What stuff?"

"You know about people recovering from COVID-19, being discharged from the hospital and then suffering effects of COVID for months, years even."

"Oh yes. They're actually calling it Long COVID. What about it?"

"I'm beginning to wonder if there could be such a thing as long trauma,"

"What? What are you on about now?"

"If there's such a thing as long trauma, don't you see that maybe that's what happened to Agnes?"

"What?"

"Her father's tragic death, maybe it affected her so much, she couldn't cope, her mind shut down until now."

"You think so?"

"I don't know! It's just a thought. Deep down, she could be missing her father, and the COVID-19 restrictions triggered a reaction."

"Like what?"

"Lockdowns, missing her mother, exam pressures, stress, anything. I don't know!"

"Well, Moira did say the home was like a student's residence sometimes."

They talked on, exchanging views, half-baked ideas, searching for something helpful, useful that they could do. It took them some time. But in the end, it was startlingly simple.

"Harry, remember what you said earlier?"

"No. What did I say?"

"You said that if Agnes is confused, mixed up etcetera, maybe she needs someone to listen to her. Someone she can trust. Someone like us. Remember?"

"So?"

"That's it, Harry. That's it, that's what we'll do. It's simple. We'll listen to her. If you're right, she's searching for something, anything, to rid her of the anxieties in her life."

Fleshing out Harry's notion, they would offer – listening ears. When Moira was working night shifts, Martha would babysit – be a presence – – in her absence, and Harry pottering around in the garden would be an afternoon presence.

Schools closed for Easter would remain closed until the third week in April. They saw little of Agnes at first. Harry pottering about in the garden would by chance be doing something by the garden gate when Agnes was going out. Oiling the hinges, screwing in a nail, anything to put himself in her way so that they would at least have to acknowledge each other. At first, that's all that happened. Then the hellos and good afternoons slowly, encounter by encounter, word by word, eased into conversations.

Harry would talk to Agnes about the roses in the bed by the gate, naming them, how to care for them, feeding, disease control, fragrances and much more. He talked about his childhood, growing up, freedom, swimming in the sea, playing football in the street, being carefree, without ambition.

"I woke up one day," he told Agnes, "when my aunt Mary took me aside. She pointed to a group of unemployed men, standing smoking at the street corner and said, 'Son, if you want to be like them boys there, it's easy, you don't have to do anything. But understand this, you wouldn't get any thanks for it, and that's all you'll be, unemployable, no use to anyone, man nor beast. Time for you to wise up son, it's your choice. Education is easily carried. It won't hurt your back, but it can take you a long way.'"

Harry, as was his way, passed seamlessly on to another topic, hoping Agnes was listening. *Even if it's going in one ear and out the other, maybe*, he thought, *it might give her something to think about later.*

When Moira was working nights, Martha babysat. It wasn't babysitting or adolescent sitting; it was mother substitution. In the evenings, Martha would encourage the girls in conversation on any topic. Agnes didn't engage. She was like a guttering candle flame, trying to avoid being snuffed out. Often she would slip away unnoticed, but Martha noticed.

Martha sought one-on-one moments with Agnes; they were hard to find. One evening Martha, for want of something to do, made an apple tart. She was taking it out of the oven when Agnes appeared in the kitchen doorway and said, "That smells good, Aunt Martha."

"Well, let's see, Agnes if it tastes good, shall we?"

"Yes, please."

"Custard, or ice cream with it, which would you like?"

"I don't know."

"Okay, while you decide, ask your sisters if they'd like a piece before we start; otherwise, there might be none left."

That was the icebreaker.

Martha was reading in the lounge when Agnes joined her. The room was tranquil; it was as if the walls were begging them to talk. Martha slowly turned the pages in her book, pretending to read. Agnes broke the silence.

"Uncle Harry was telling me what it was like when he was growing up. What was it like for you, Aunt Martha?"

"Nothing much to tell, dear," Martha answered, hoping to draw the girl into more questions. It was a risk, but it worked.

"What about school?"

"It was demolished years ago. There's a car park there now. That's progress, I suppose."

"Did you like school?"

"Some things I liked, others I didn't. It changed with the seasons, subjects and teachers, I suppose."

"What subjects?"

"The three 'Rs', reading, writing and arithmetic. It didn't fire my imagination. There was little aspirational about it."

"Were you unhappy?"

"I don't know if I was happy or not. I was too young, you see. I told my mother once that I didn't want to go to school anymore."

"What did she say?"

"She said, 'think about it, dear.' She was busy with a line of washing at the time. Bad timing on my part, looking back on it. But I did think about it a lot. All I saw was the factory, my future, looming at the end of the street."

"Did you work in a factory, Aunt Martha?"

"No, I didn't. One of my teachers, a lovely kind old lady, found out, from my mother I suspect, that I didn't want to go back to school. She sent for me. Asked me what the problem was. I told her I didn't see the point of it all, as I would end up in the factory anyway. 'Child,' she said, 'you have the ability, but you lack ambition. What do you want to be when you leave school?'

"It was the first time I was asked what I wanted to be. I couldn't answer; I had no idea what I wanted to be. 'Come back to school, think about it, decide, talk to me, and we'll find a way for you.' Funny, I can remember what she said word for word. So I went back to school, and the rest is history. My world back then, love, was very different from yours today."

Agnes, digesting everything Martha said, didn't seek clarification or amplification. Martha was relieved. They sat in mutual silence, measured only by the ticking mantle clock. Agnes, after a little while, clearing her throat, apologetically said, "Thank you, Aunt Martha. I didn't mean to pry, goodnight."

"You didn't, dear, goodnight."

Martha delved into her book, wondering why she'd told Agnes about not wanting to go back to school.

As Martha and Harry rallied around Moira's family, the government combated Covid-19. The 2021 University Boat race was moved from its usual venue on the River Thames in London. Then it emerged that the Scientific Advisory Group for Emergencies (SAGE) couldn't calculate an R number for the whole of the UK and that a COVID passport scheme would be trialled in Liverpool. An Office for National Statistics' survey suggested that 1 in 5 people had Long COVID five weeks after their initial infection and that 1 in 7 still had it after twelve weeks. On the upside, record numbers of second doses of vaccines were administered.

The thought of schools reopening after Easter was like a time bomb ticking inside Moira. She had tried to talk to Agnes several times about her reasons for not going back to college. They were difficult conversations in which Agnes repeated her mantra. Moira, listening patiently, counselled her daughter. Agnes was left in no doubt that she didn't have to study medicine or work in the NHS if she didn't want to and that she had a life of opportunity; it was hers to take. Moira cautioned Agnes that there were no shortcuts to growing up, but there were many different routes to get there and that her choice now would shape her future. Counselled and cautioned, Agnes, considered her options.

It was Saturday afternoon, the weekend before schools reopened. Moira had invited Martha and Harry over for coffee. Agnes, in her quiet diminutive way, joined them. Closing the lounge door, she stood momentarily composing herself. When she stopped fidgeting, the deep well of love in her young heart found expression in words.

"Mum," she said, "I want to go back to college. I'll try very hard. I promise. Okay? I'm sorry for what I did and what I said. I...I..I don't know what made me do it?"

Silence flooded the lounge. It was unbearable. But the room was bursting with relief. Moira, smiling, stood up, walked over and embraced Agnes, saying,

"You don't have to be sorry, Agnes. Maybe I gave you good cause."

She was gently caressing Agnes's shoulders when Martha and Harry joined them to form a four-person huddle. On the way home, Harry said, "It's not over yet for Agnes, Martha; we'll know better by the May-June midterm break."

Harry was in the garden when Agnes came home from school the first day back after Easter, and he thought there was the hint of a bounce in her step. "How's it going, Agnes?"

"All right."

"There's something special I found in the garden that I want to show you."

Agnes, a question wrinkling her brow, followed Harry to a small patch of unmown grass.

"Do you see them?"

"See what?"

"Look closer."

The patch of grass, was no bigger than a tea towel. Bending over it, Agnes exclaimed, "I see them, six, no, nine of them, little blue and white flowers. What are they, Uncle Harry?"

"They're wild orchids, Agnes. I think this is the common spotted orchid. Why don't you Google it."

"They're beautiful; I didn't know they were there."

"Folk cut their grass without looking or thinking most of the time, and little gems like these are lost. Anyway, we'll leave them be. There's much to see all around us if we would only look."

"They're amazing. I'll Google them," she promised, bouncing away from the orchids.

In May, Moira was back on night shift duty. Martha was alone in the lounge reflecting on Manley Hopkins's poem, 'The May Magnificat'. It was the line, 'Why fasten that upon her' that Martha pondered, thinking about Agnes.

Why fasten anything on anybody? We all do it. Don't we? We can't help seeing people in black and white, no shades of grey, mercilessly burdening them in our chattering, with faults and failings.

Agnes, interrupting her thoughts, said, "Hot chocolate for two, Aunt Martha?"

Martha thought that was a great idea.

Placing a tray on the coffee table, Agnes said, "Hot chocolate with chocolate cake?"

"Don't tell Harry, Agnes."

"Mum made it today."

"Delicious Agnes."

"What have you been doing, Aunt Martha, during the pandemic?"

In a non-sequential, disjointed kind of way, Martha told Agnes everything that she and Harry had been doing and were still doing.

"You're writing short stories and learning Italian? That's amazing."

"Not really. We were keeping our minds active and entertaining ourselves writing little memoirs. Reminiscences. You know little tales from memory. It was easy, and it was fun. We had some great laughs, I can tell you. Then I made the mistake of suggesting we write a made-up story about something we came across on one of our walks. That's when our writing found a new edge. It was tough for me. We worked at our story for nearly a month before we had something readable. Can you believe it, Agnes? It was hard work."

"Yes, I can believe it. One of my 'O' Levels is in English Literature, and it's tough going."

"I don't doubt it. Writing readable stuff isn't easy."

"Can I read your story? What's it called?"

"Of course you can. It's called the ditched van in Killyglen. So long as you tell me what you think of it."

"Tu parli l'italiano?"Agnes asked.

"Si,un po, e tu?"

"Si. Sto studiando l'italiano."

They conversed in Italian a little until it was time to say, 'Buono Notte.' That night Martha slept well. Conversation conduits with Agnes were opening up.

In May, lockdown restrictions lessened further. Hotels were opened, indoor hospitality was revived, rules affecting outdoor social contact were removed, and more people were allowed to meet indoors. Suddenly it seemed the UK was in a brighter, freer mood. Holiday mania, though atmospheric, didn't taint the air Martha and Harry breathed. They remained guarded.

The feedback from Agnes on Martha's short story was cheerful and helpful. They talked about the different types of short storeys; comedy, tragedy, drama, adventure, mystery and love. A general story about some everyday occurrence incorporating different themes was also a possibility, Agnes suggested. She stressed the importance of text structure, plot development and the context in which the story was set in informing the reader; using her edits to Martha's white van story to illustrate what she meant. It was too much, too academic for Martha to absorb all at once. It was for Martha like being on the receiving end of a one-on-one master class in story writing. Agnes, sensing Martha's discomfort, suggested she think about what they had discussed, perhaps talk it over with Uncle Harry and see where it takes us. Martha noted the inclusivity of the little word *us*.

Martha and Agnes also spent time together cooking Italian dishes and conversing in Italian. Confidences grew. Agnes relaxed a little, slowly unfolding like Harry's orchids in the garden and beginning to talk about herself and how she felt. Martha listened.

Her schoolwork was slipping, difficulty sleeping, feeling helpless, constantly tired and mixed up. How she worried about her mum, working so hard, giving so much, risking her life every time she went into the hospital. Listening earnestly, Martha heard Agnes whisper she was afraid of losing her mother too; it was a murmured confession. If Martha hadn't been caringly listening, she would have missed the adverb, too. The volume of meaning that little word possessed was revelatory.

"Don't worry, pet," Martha said, you won't be losing her, and we won't be losing you. Ok? Let's see if this bacon, broccoli and parmesan pasta was worth our efforts."

As lockdown restrictions continued to ease, Moira informed her line manager of her need to work day shifts, four days a week.

The government decided that the proposed end of social contact restrictions on the 21st of June would be delayed until the third week in July. The vaccination roll-out would be accelerated following concerns of new variants of the coronavirus being more transmissible. Daily confirmed cases in the third wave of the pandemic continued to rise. Confirmed cases peaked at over 50,000 per day. Pressures on the NHS surged.

Moira's employers refused her request to work a four-day week. She immediately registered with a nursing employment agency, resolved to leave the NHS if a suitable job arose. Explaining her decision to Martha and Harry, she said, "I was so involved in my work that I lost sight of my family. That's not something to clap about and be proud of...is it?"

"Sleep on it, Moira."

"I don't need to, Martha. My mind's made up."

"Why don't you talk it over with your daughters?"

"What for.?"

"Well, they might have something to say about it."

"What can they say? It's something I have to deal with."

"They might tell you they admire you, love you, and are worried sick about you. They might even tell you they know you're saving people's lives."

"You think so? Sometimes I forget they're adults."

Suddenly from nowhere, it was summer, schools had closed, and it was vacation time. For Moira, her girls, and Martha and Harry, it was staycation time, which for Martha and Harry meant staying at home; going anywhere was too risky.

It was a Sunday afternoon. Moira was with her daughters in the lounge, spending the afternoon together. Moira waited for the right moment, – an interlude in conversation, to inform them as casually as she could, of the lifestyle changes she intended to make. When the moment came, Moira wasn't casual and didn't avail of the colours on her palette when ministering to her patients. She was unintentionally blunt. Her colours were black and white.

"Girls," she said, commanding their attention, "there's something I have to tell you."

They looked at her, uncertainty showing in their eyes.

"I have decided to leave the NHS as soon as I can find another job."

Silence filled the room as her daughters looked one to the other, absorbing the import of their mother's declaration.

"Wh… Why?" her eldest daughter enquired.

"Because it has become too much for me. Too demanding."

"You work too much, Mum. You don't have to. Do you?"

"The NHS is under an awful lot of pressure. It's full-on twenty-four seven. You've no idea what it's like."

"But you have to look after yourself, Mum. You're no use to the NHS if you burn yourself out. Are you?" Megan questioned.

"None at all. Only another burden." Moira laughing, hoping to ease their concerns.

"Why don't you work days instead of nights all the time?"

"It's complicated, and we're so short-staffed. I asked to work a four day week, but my request was refused."

"I don't believe it. How could they? You've given your life to nursing. You're not giving up nursing. Are you?" Denise wanted to know.

"No. But I want to spend more time with you. Absorbed in my work, I lost sight of you."

"You did nothing of the sort. We know what you were doing." Megan retorted, looking at her sisters for support. "You were saving people's lives. We're proud of you. Lots of families would have lost loved ones but for you and your colleagues. That's something to be proud of. Isn't it? You are appreciated and admired. We are proud of you!"

"And I'm proud of you too. Now when I think of the danger, I was exposing you to coming home shift after shift, tired out fighting the virus." Moira responded, "I could ..."

"Well, you didn't. We worried about you too, Mum, you know," Denise added,

"I...I.. I was afraid of leaving you, being taken by the virus. I couldn't sleep thinking about what you would do and..." Moira's voice died in her throat.

They sat in thoughtful silence. Raw, buried feelings, deeply felt, openly shared. The summer sun had moved westwards. The lounge's brilliant brightness had lost its intensity. Shadows stretched from under the bow window across the entire width of the lawn.

Sitting close by her mother, Agnes pierced the silence, "I was afraid of losing you too, mummy."

"I know Agnes. I know, my love," Moira comforted, feeling the fear and pain radiating from her child. She sat, letting the moment linger, then stood up, extending her open arms inviting her daughters home. Hugging each other, tears of joy and relief washed away their concerns and anxieties

The pandemic hadn't gone away. Society, it seemed, had taken a breather and relaxed. In hospitals, it was a different story. COVID-19 admissions increased, ICUs were full, younger people were being admitted to hospital, COVID related deaths increased, and Health Trusts, coping with extreme pressures, appealed for off duty staff to return to work. Slowly an ominous cloud of uneasiness settled over high streets, the hustle and bustle of business waned, people went about their business circumspectly. Waiting?

Moira and Agnes's reconciliation raised Martha and Harrys' spirits. They felt very hopeful. It was as if they had left a patch of shade and walked into the gentle, warming morning sunlight. Martha and Harry continued their routines. Agnes joined them on their walks and excursions of discovery. They found quirky things to photograph and write about. Agnes enthusiastically facilitated their fictional endeavours, focusing their attention on how to tell their storeys. Her suggested edits they found particularly helpful. Too often, they would include extraneous material and use too many words. As summer waned, their storeys markedly improved.

In September, schools reopened, Agnes was back in college, her sisters back in university, and her mother still worked in the NHS. There was no drama surrounding Agnes's return to school. She was good in herself, energised. It was where she wanted to be. She'd had taken her first jab without having to be asked twice. But there was confusion and chaos; test and trace resulted in thousands of children being sent home to self-isolate following close contact with a COVID-19 positive person.

The government announced its autumn and winter strategy for tackling Covid; Plans A and B. Plan A relied on the promotion of vaccines and testing to prevent the NHS from being overwhelmed. Unvaccinated citizens would be encouraged to get vaccinated. Vaccines would be offered to children twelve to fifteen years of age, and a booster jab programme for millions would be introduced within weeks. Testing and tracing would continue, as would self-isolation for anyone catching the virus. Businesses would be encouraged to consider using the NHS Covid Pass to admit patrons.

Plan B to be enacted if further measures were needed to protect the NHS included; urging the public to act more cautiously, the use of mandatory vaccine passports for mass events, mandatory use of face coverings and guidance on working from home.

Harry listening attentively, for once, to the prime minister's press conference, thought, *they're getting desperate. It's all about avoiding another lockdown. Don't people get it yet? Covid-19 is here to stay.*

The number of children absent in state schools due to COVID-19 rose alarmingly in September. By the end of the month, over 200,000 children were registered absent from school. Alarm bells rang around the UK. The Prime Minister offered the country succour, reassuring that Christmas 2021 would be better than last. Concerns over rising cases of COVID-19 in schoolchildren continued unabated. The new Delta Covid-19 mutant was surging. Hospital admissions were up 10%. Daily reported Covid-19 cases had exceeded 50,000 for the first time in months. A hospital trust declared a COVID related critical incident. The British Medical Association called on the government to act now. Hints of nervous trepidations in government circles emerged. Morocco banned flights from the UK.

In their *Coronavirus: Lessons Learned to Date Report*, the House of Commons Health and Social Care and Science and Technology Committees highlighted that the government's preparedness to deal with influenza was insufficient to combat Covid-19. Lessons had not been learned from outbreaks of SARS and MERS in Asian countries in recent years.

Martha and Harry received their booster and flu jabs at the end of October. There were no side effects this time for Martha. But acutely aware of Covid-19's increasing prevalence in society and mounting pressures to ease restrictions, particularly in hospitality, they didn't let their guard drop.

"It doesn't make sense to me, Martha. Going into the church, we hand sanitise, social distance, and provide contact details for test and trace purposes. We wear face coverings, and the pews are sanitised too. It's a big airy space. Now they're going to allow nightclubs to open. No requirement for social distancing, wearing face-coverings and all the rest of it. Can you credit it? Can you explain it to me?"

"No, Harry. I don't understand it."

"Did you hear the latest? They've discovered that even if you're double vaccinated, you can get the virus and pass it on."

"That's awful."

"It's not over yet, Martha. Far from it."

On All Hallows Eve, it dawned on Martha that Christmas was fast approaching, and they were, unlike previous years, unprepared. Harry, head down working on his laptop, glanced up at Martha when she spoke, "Harry, you know it's almost Christmas?" Her anxious tone seized his attention.

Pausing, he answered, "Yes."

"We haven't done anything."

"There's no hurry, and sure we're not going anywhere."

"What about our family?"

"What about them?"

"Have you told Deidre we're not going to Edinburgh?"

"Not yet."

"Do it now, Harry, please and log off. I need to talk to you."

Martha and Harry concluded that it would be best if they shared all-day Christmas Eve with their children; one family at a time, via video linkages, Harry would arrange to suit everyone. The arrangement would leave everyone unfettered to enjoy Christmas Day. It would also leave Martha and Harry free on Christmas Eve to participate in the live televised midnight Mass from Saint Peter's Basilica in Rome. They also decided to invite Moira and her daughters to join them for lunch on Christmas Day. But before they could action their invitation, Martha and Harry received in their morning post a beautiful hand-crafted card inviting them to share Christmas lunch with Moira, Denise, Megan, and Agnes.

On Christmas night, Martha and Harry left Moira and her daughters at nine o'clock to make their way home. They were happy and contented; Moira and her daughters were happy and contented too, and Martha and Harrys' family had grown.

Chaine Memorial Road, stretching its length beside the languid sea, was silent and empty when they turned in from Tower Road and parked outside their house. The night was still, and nothing moved. It wasn't cold. Above them, a blanket of soft greyish cloud covered the town blocking out the light from distant stars. There was something eerie about the silent, empty street almost smothered in cloud hovering patiently above the chimney pots.

Martha shivered as they made their way from the car to their front door. The house looked empty. Entering, unlike the home they had just left, it felt empty. It was to them momentarily like a bird's nest when the chicks had fledged and left. When they have gone, the parent birds leave too. The nest had served its purpose; it isn't needed anymore; it's not a home. Next spring, they'll make a nest somewhere else. Wherever takes their fancy. Martha and Harry, unlike birds, were fixed in place in their nest; they would not, could not abandon it. Their nest was comfortably warm and habitable because Harry had set the central heating clock to turn the heating on at seven o'clock. It was their home of many memories.

Martha and Harry sat together in the front room; the only light, a reading lamp on a small table nestled beside the fireplace, looking out the window across the silent street over the quiet black rolling sea, sipping their favourite nightcap. Harry thinking aloud broke the silence asking, "What do you think this world will be like fifty years from now?"

Martha, eyes on the sea, just shook her head.

A few flaky shadows made Harry look twice. It was snowing. Giant, soft, delicate crystals floated unhurriedly down to earth, gliding through the glow of the amber street light onto the waiting asphalt surfaces below. Soon everything, roads, pavements, gardens, bushes, trees and rooftops would be reshaped by gently, faintly, falling flakes of snow.

The morning would resonate with the delightful shrieking sounds of children running around foot-printing, and building snowmen in the Bay Field behind them. Memories filled the hearts of Martha and Harry.

With nothing left to do, they looked forward to the dawning of another New Year.

They hadn't heard of Omicron – yet.

A Wakening

From the blackness of my night,
Dawning heralds Your loving light.
Afraid to breathe at my surprise,
Your nearness fills my tired eyes.
Another day exerts its tug
I look at You smile and shrug,
Tomorrow's just another day.

The People You Meet

"If I live until 2040, I'll be a hundred," Anne Marie told her mirror image. Appraising herself, back, front, sideways, and from top to toe, the thought pleased her.

"You've got to be particular about how you dress when going out; sure, you never know who you're going to meet," she reminded herself.

Anne Marie wasn't vain, quite the contrary she would have insisted. But she had an abundance of self-respect, which on rare occasions flirted with the boundaries of self-conceit.

In the full-length hall mirror, studying herself through small greenish-blue eyes, she stood five feet three and a half inches tall, weighed about one hundred and twenty pounds, with an apologetic nose and a thin mouth. Her lipstick-free lips creased her freckled face. She had fought a losing battle with her hair. Her once lustrous black curly locks had gradually lost their curls, straightened and turned dull grey.

Stepping back from the mirror, she took another self-appraising look. Her stout black leather shoes, tailored black slacks, black zip-fastened jacket with oversized lapels, deep pink brimmed woollen bonnet with matching long woollen scarf draping her shoulders, she looked and felt good to go.

The first total lockdown had been in summer. It was warm then, and the days were long, with lots to do and much to enjoy in the garden. People she encountered on her walks were light-hearted, free and unencumbered. Hope, gilded with the promise of better times ahead, lightened the air.

The second lockdown was different. It was winter; days were short, overcast, dreary and bleak. Time had slowed. Her once vibrant street was dull and uninviting. The neighbourhood was socially barren; there was little to do, and the garden was dreary. With her two children, isolating and working from home, the house had become cell-like, entrapping. But tarnished hope, bolstered with self-reliance, proffered a practical way forward. She had to get out, feel the fresh sea breeze on her face, find herself again.

Satisfied that her appearance met the demands of self-respect, Anne Marie sallied forth on her usual morning walk, down Curran Road, Bay Road, and along Chaine Memorial Road, with the prospect of seeing the '*Stranraer*' boat, threading its way in or out of the harbour. Anne Marie would casually survey Island-magee, pass the 'Chaine Tower', with her keen eyes alert for anything interesting in the sea, on to the promenade, and then up and down through the parks, out to the Black Arch where she would finally turn and stroll back home.

At Waterloo Bay she always hoped to see the curlew, a brief, infrequent encounter, the highlight of her walk because her presence, unlike the curlew's, wasn't tidal dependent.

On the promenade, passing the leisure centre, Anne Marie heard a vaguely familiar voice speak her name from out of the sea mist.

Who is that? Anne Marie asked herself, *I know that voice.*

Desperately trying to put a face to the voice, she heard it again.

"Anne Marie, how are you doing? I haven't seen you in a long time?"

"Cecil?... Cecil? Is that you, Cecil?" she queried, squinting towards the voice.

He was a few metres away and getting closer. It was Cecil. He was wearing a dull-looking windcheater, matching jeans, a peaked cloth cap on his head and trainers on his feet.

A long time ago, they met in The Kings Arms hotel ballroom, on a Saturday night, when he asked her to dance. Anne Marie and Cecil's sister went to the same school and worked together in a local solicitor's office before Anne Marie chose a career in nursing. On Saturday nights that followed, Anne Marie and Cecil often danced together. They became friends, enjoying ice creams between dances. This chance encounter was their first since Anne Marie's husband died just over two years ago. It was just like yesterday, her pain still raw.

Her husband Bert and Cecil had been part of a group of lads back in the day that danced Anne Marie and her girlfriends on Saturday nights in the Kings Arms. Thoughts of those Saturday nights flashed across her mind as they spoke. A tall, lanky man, Cecil spoke with a soft drawl that always reminded her of James Stewart, the film actor. He was gentle, kind and there was a tranquillity about him that made her feel safe. Though fond of each other, they never dated; he didn't ask, and she didn't push. *There was a shyness about him, about both of us perhaps,* she thought. Though she would later think of their relationship as platonic, she often wondered, *what if?* She fell in love and married Bert, and Cecil didn't marry. It never occurred to Anne Marie to wonder why.

Anne Marie, keeping her distance, apologising said,

"Cecil, I didn't recognise you for a moment. It's been a long time. How are you? It's great to get out for a walk, isn't it ?"

"Lovely to see you, Anne Marie." Cecil said, leaning towards her. "Yes, you're right, it's good to talk!"

"What have you been doing with yourself?" Anne Marie continued.

"Still on the shelf, Anne Marie, auch sure you never know, chance would be a fine thing."

Anne Marie, a little unsure of herself, quietly asked, "Are you alright, Cecil?"

"What?" Cecil queried.

Left foot first, he stepped closer; she instinctively, on her right foot, stepped back. As Cecil moved sideways to the right, she moved sideways to the left. Feet together, he paused, and they reset. They started again. He led left foot first, she followed, continuing their crab-like movement and disconnected, disjointed conversation until they turned through one hundred and eighty degrees.

"We must keep our social distance, you know, Cecil!" Anne Marie advised.

Stepping towards her again, left foot first, Cecil admitted, "I don't do much socialising now, you know."

Anne Marie, right foot stepping backwards and moving to the left as he moved to the right, said just a little irritably, "I think we've got off on the wrong foot Cecil, don't you think?"

"I don't drink anymore, Anne Marie, gave all that up, a long time ago, you know."

They circled each other three or four times in waltz time to a kind of one-two-three, awkward rhythm. It wasn't a Fred Astaire, Ginger Rodgers well-rehearsed, beautifully executed routine. It was a discordant, staccato, unrehearsed dance of the deaf. But Anne Marie didn't know that. As they pranced around, she wondered, *am I dreaming this? Is this some kind of pantomime? Is it a comic operetta or what?*

All kinds of disharmonious thoughts played around in her head until she realised they were heading back the way she'd come and that if they kept on going, she would soon be back home. Exasperated, Anne Marie stopped, thrust her left arm out full stretch, the palm of her hand towards Cecil, forcing him to halt.

"What is the matter with you, Cecil?" she addressed him as she would a disobedient child.

"What?" Cecil, a hand to his ear, asked.

The raising of the cupped hand to the ear alerted Anne Marie, "What? … What are you saying Cecil, I don't understand?"

Sheepishly, Cecil admitted, "I can't hear you very well. I have to wear hearing aids now, you know, but I forgot to put them in today."

"You what? Do you realise you're putting yourself and others, including me, at risk? We're dancing around here like a couple of idiots! What if anyone had seen us?" Anne Marie testily responded,

"Who's Iris?" Cecil muttered.

Dancing, Anne Marie realised, is what we're doing: dancing the *'box step'* we used to do in the King Arms years ago.

Anger writhed in her chest like a coiled rattlesnake waiting to strike. *How could he not wear his dammed hearing aids? She liked Cecil, don't hurt him; we're not in a confined space,* she reasoned with herself. She was aware that virus transmission could be airborne, and she was upwind; moving a little closer to Cecil, she spoke louder. The social distance between them had grown with time, but the physical distance between them now was less than two metres. Outdoors and upwind, I'm safe enough, Anne Marie figured. She calmed, regained her composure and happily chatted about the times they spent together at the dances until they ran out of things to say.

"Until we meet again, Cecil, I think we've danced enough for one day. Perhaps another time," Anne Marie said laughing.

Blessed big dim-witted dumbbell, she thought as his hunched shoulders faded from view. *How do friends lose each other?* The thought saddened her.

Feeling light-headed, Anne Marie leant on the promenade guard rail, her mind in turmoil. The heavy rolling waves bullied the sea wall below. Her throbbing heart pumped pulses of blood through her arteries as she thought of Cecil, Covid-19 unaware, strolling towards her carefree, unconcerned, unafraid, at ease with himself, wishing she could be just a little like that.

Why do I have to be so serious? If only I'd worn my glasses, I would have seen him coming, and I'd have had time to prepare. Anne Marie asked herself.

For the first time in five years, she wished she had a cigarette – something to draw on – inhale.

Why didn't I wear my glasses? What did I get them for? Questions pillaged her reasoning as she frantically rummaged in her bag for her spectacles. Her pocketed hand clasped a rosary, and fingering the beads; she mouthed a litany of prayers until her inner self calmed. Opening her eyes, she saw the sea had quietened too. It was that moment of calm between ebb and flow. Glasses now firmly planted on the bridge of her nose, she continued her walk, thinking, *I'll wear my face mask outside from now on too. It's getting too risky.*

Nearing the winding path leading up to the Town Park, she noticed an elderly woman some distance away pushing a pram towards her. She wasn't walking. The woman was hirpling. Anne Marie's heart rushed out to her; she was looking after somebody's child, maybe a grandchild or even a great-grandchild. When her caring nature took over, Anne Marie's imagination knew no boundaries; she could justify behaviours that others might reasonably construe as interference. *What should I do?* She wondered. The question of why she should feel the need to do anything didn't cross her mind. *I wonder if she needs any help? No harm in asking, is there?* She convinced herself, completely ignoring the possibility, that an independently minded elderly lady might resent being thought of as someone in need of help.

Like a predator, she closed in, noting in the process that the person she was bearing down on was not best dressed for a winter's morning. The path down from the park branched left and right to join the promenade. Anne Marie was opposite the left branch by the railing. Further along, the old lady was stationary at the right branch. Hunched over the pram, Anne Marie thought, she's making the baby more comfortable, but Anne Marie was mistaken. She's lifting the baby out of the pram, but she is mistaken again. Getting closer, Anne Marie realised it wasn't a baby! It was a tiny dog, a Chihuahua. It wasn't a pram she was pushing either; it was one of those three-wheeled walking aids older people use with a fitted pouch to put bits and pieces in. In this case, a dog. From the pouch, she produced a lead, clipped it to the dog's collar and fastened the other end onto her three-wheeler.

It has a better gait than you, missus, Anne Marie unkindly thought. Then a chorus of discordant thoughts entered her mind; *perhaps she's living alone, the wee dog is the only friend she's got, what can I do for her? Is there anything the woman needs? Does she have a family?* A voice interrupted her thoughts. The woman was speaking to her.

"Are you all right, love? She inquired, concern etching her weathered face. You look a bit under the weather, dear. Are you ok?"

"I'm fine, thank you," Anne Marie managed, how are you?"

"There's not a bother on me, love, thank God. Me and Charlie," she said, referring to her dog, "take a walk every day hail, rain or snow, he needs it, you know, he's getting on a bit. He's troubled with arthritis in his little legs, poor thing. Sure you can't sit in all day, dear, can you? It would drive you up the walls, wouldn't it? Even he gets restless," she said, pointing to Charlie.

They chatted about the lockdown and the pandemic, in general, exchanging anecdotes until parting, the elderly woman said, "Enjoy your day, dear and look after yourself now, won't you? We all need to do that, don't we?"

She went on her way, dog in tow, leaving Anne Marie wondering what she saw in her that prompted the question, are you all right, love? *Why* Anne Marie wondered, *am I drawn to someone I think is in need? Is this a kind of need-love syndrome in reverse? Am I emotionally impoverished? I'm not a child needing mother comfort. I had a happy childhood, happy, fulfilled marriage, and a happy family. What is it then? Loneliness? I'm not lonely. I've loads of friends. Maybe it's lockdown syndrome.*

This behavioural trait surfaced when she retired. She would instantly react when her phone or doorbell rang at home as if it was an emergency. Anne Marie was retired officially, but perhaps she couldn't get the job and the responsibility that went with it out of her system. Anne Marie wasn't clinging on; it was as if the job wouldn't let her go! She had gone to help an old woman who didn't need help, in the process discovering that she was the one thought to be needing help. Shaking her head, she gave herself a-get-a-grip-on-yourself-nudge and walked on.

Anne Marie didn't get far. A chain-linked barrier erected after a rock fall caused by the heavy rainfall denied progress along the promenade. Fair enough, Anne Marie thought, shrugging irritably. She was about to turn around when two jogging youths passed her, and without changing stride stepped nimbly up onto the promenade railing, grabbed the barrier with both hands, swung around it, dropped down on the other side and continued happily on their way. Anne Marie knew it was wrong, reckless perhaps, but she had to applaud their light-hearted disregard of the impediment in their way. She couldn't help wishing she could do the same, but those days were long gone, she knew. Smiling, Anne Marie retraced her steps and made her way up the winding path to the Town Park.

Halfway up, she paused; her arthritis had kicked in. *I know how the Chihuahua feels,* she thought, regretting not taking her medication, telling herself, *you never learn, do you?* Anne Marie had an aversion to taking medication of any kind unless absolutely necessary. But as she often discovered, there was a cost, and this was one of those occasions. Standing, with the park behind her looking out over the sea, she heard a voice speak,

"Anne Marie, is that yourself? I haven't seen you in a long time. How're you doing?" Before she could turn around, the voice continued. "You know you're the first person I've spoken to in a week. I haven't been out of the house, the weather was that bad, and I wasn't feeling too good."

"Robby, it's yourself," she said, facing him, but he continued like a running tap.

"You're looking well for your age. It must be all the walking you're doing, but be careful; too much of a good thing can be a bad thing," he said, laughing at his joke.

Anne Marie laughed too, thinking, this is what lockdown does to people. He's so starved of company that he's bubbling away like a simmering casserole. Robby talked on hardly taking a breath, about looking forward to spring, what seeds he would sow, shrubs he had to shift and other bits and pieces that occupied his compartmented mind in lockdown. Then abruptly, he said, "Well, I've detained you long enough; better be on my way, enjoy your walk."

Stepping off the path onto the grass in deference, she said, "Robby, do you mind when we were children we used to run up and down here and swim in the sea?"

Turning and looking back up at her, smiling, he said, "Happy days, Anne Marie, It wasn't yesterday, was it? That was a day or two ago."

She watched him go. All he had wanted, needed was a listening ear to hear his inner voice, and he had both of hers.

"Was that need-love or just a bit of need-company?" she asked herself. Smiling, Anne Marie, her arthritis forgotten, floated up the path into the park.

People with dogs were gathering. Anne Marie did a couple of laps around what used to be the football pitch. Now ball games were prohibited if tossing balls for dogs to retrieve wasn't considered a ball game. Sign of the times, she thought, making her way towards Chaine's Park. The narrow path linking the two parks was less than a metre wide. A young woman pushing a pram approached. Without a second thought, Anne Marie stepped off the path onto the muddied grass to give way. The young woman acknowledging her smiled a thank you, to which Anne Marie responded cheerily, "You're welcome."

Then she saw a big burly man, pulled along by two aggressive-looking dogs, heading her way. Okay, she calculated it's either their eight paws and his two big feet or her two wee feet to be muddied. Anne Marie decided enough was enough. It was time to make a stand. A decision that was a long time in the brewing. She was not deferring anymore to dogs and their handlers. They closed on each other. She tensed. Had she the guts to face them down? Could she hold her nerve? Fight her corner? What if it was a standoff? Suddenly her OK Corral moment had come! There could be no chickening out now. Then the big burly man, deferring to Anne Marie, smiling stepped off the path onto the muddy grass taking his dogs with him. Anne Marie grudgingly forced an ungracious thank you through tightly compressed lips as man and dogs unperturbed went on their way.

Anne Marie marched out of Chaine's Park onto the Coast Road, heading north.

"Why did I have to be so confrontational," she asked herself.

"Because I wanted to," she retorted.

"But you're afraid of dogs," her other voice countered.

'So what? Be a doormat, and people and dogs will walk all over you."

"You'd like that wouldn't you?"

"No, I wouldn't. I'd think more of myself. I'm tired of deferring to folk with their dogs on the pavement, especially men. You think it's right I step off the pavement onto a busy road, put myself at risk while they and their dogs domineer the pavement?"

"It's not the dog's fault," her other self told her.

"I know it bloody well isn't, do you think I'm that stupid?"

The furious internal debate raged inside her head, all the way to the Black Arch before it began to subside. Mentally and physically exhausted, Anne Marie slowed down, turned and headed for home. In a blind rage, she hadn't seen or acknowledged anyone on the way north. Heading back, meeting people, Anne Marie wondered if she'd shamed herself in any way. Hugging the railings and fixedly staring at the dispassionate sea offered no comfort.

Approaching Chaine's Park, she peeled off the Coast Road down to the promenade. The path took her past Waterloo Bay with the prospect, the tide being on the turn, of seeing her favourite bird, the curlew. It was Anne Marie's lucky day. She saw a pair of curlews earnestly wading together, using their long curved beaks foraging for food until disturbed by children and dogs took flight and left. A calmness had settled on her. She loved this little oasis, set innocuously in millions of years of earth's history amidst the humdrum of everyday life.

Ambling on, she was overtaken by a man, a woman and a child. There was nothing remarkable about them. They were followed by a man and his dog and a cyclist, a proper cyclist with lycra gear and an expensive lightweight bicycle. Then she noticed the threesome had halted. They couldn't go any further. A barrier similar to the one she had encountered on her way out blocked their way.

Undeterred, the man scrambled up the steep, grassy bank. The woman passed the child up to him. Clutching the child he scrambled around the barrier, and down the other side to deposit the child on the promenade. He then clambered back up the steep grassy bank to help the woman negotiate the barrier and together they sprauchaled down onto the promenade where the child was waiting.

Anne Marie, open-mouthed, watched the whole farce unfold. But there was more. The man with his dog followed suit, taking his cue from those ahead of him. The cyclist shouldered his bike and followed too. "What is it with people?" Anne Marie asked herself, "is it herd instinct? Are we all lemmings?" She might have felt like applauding the carefree youthful joggers defeating the other barrier earlier, but this was different; it was to her mind very different. It was mind-bogglingly reckless. *Why do people do it? Is it a challenge? An obstacle to be overcome? Have they no sense? It's the same in shops, people not wearing face coverings in a pandemic.* Shaking her head in disbelief, Anne Marie turned to tackle the seventy-four stone steps she called Jacob's Ladder that climbed to the top of Chaine's Park.

As she climbed, she noticed that the stone steps formed linked stairs. Fourteen in all. It was a moment of revelation. Jacob's ladder had become her Via Dolorosa, the way of the cross. Each stair, a station of the cross. At the top of the park, she turned and looked back down the stone steps that would be forever her Via Dolorosa, something new and uplifting to look forward to on her daily walks. Contented in mind and soul, she made her way into the Town Park, paused behind the curved granite stone wall at the top of the Bank Heads and gazed out over the sea below. The morning sea mist had lifted. Patches of water glistened under the weak sun forcing her to shield her eyes. She hadn't met anyone and was glad of that. She'd had enough for one day.

She walked into town to purchase some items for the casserole she was going to cook. The little rucksack on her back was big enough to hold her few purchases. Masked up, she entered the supermarket; it wasn't busy. She made her selections and, as usual, ended up with more than was needed. At the checkout, she discovered her Visa card was at home, where she'd left it, for safekeeping, of course, but she had cash. Except that when everything was totalled at the checkout, she was three pounds fifty-three pence short. A frantic search through her pockets and the rucksack failed to unearth more cash. Pragmatic as ever, Anne Marie asked for the three pounds fifty pence worth of items to be deleted to complete her purchase. All the while, a queue built up behind her, and she was acutely conscious of it.

"Oh don't do that, let me help you," a voice behind her said.

From behind two impatient gentlemen, a tiny old lady reached over and pushed a five-pound note into the cashier's hand; there was a moment's hesitation before Anne Marie unfroze and tried unsuccessfully to refuse the old lady's generosity.

Anne Marie waited to thank her properly as she exited the checkout.

"It was nothing," the old lady said. "Sure wouldn't you have done the same for me?"

All the way home, Anne Marie wondered, *would I? Would I have been so spontaneously generous?* She was trained to respond in emergencies. The old lady's response to her need didn't come from training; it was an act of gift-love. Innate.

Anne Marie's walk home was uneventful until she turned into her street. The day was fading fast. The road was sullen and empty, except for a neighbour walking towards her. Jim, her next-door neighbour, one removed, a bachelor, living alone. Although she hadn't seen him for almost a week, Anne Marie would have been content to acknowledge him with a wave, but he crossed the street to talk to her. After banal neighbourly exchanges, Jim smiled and said, "I've been diagnosed with cancer. It's serious."

Before Anne Marie could even think about how to respond, Jim continued, "The good news is my consultant rang to tell me to be ready for surgery sometime in the next two weeks. That's great, isn't it?"

Anne Marie was reeling in a confusion of thoughts. She knew better than Jim what lay ahead of him. Bolstering, she told him it was fortunate in the middle of a lockdown that treatment was available, harbouring the thought that his condition must be severe while saying it was good they had caught it so soon. Surprisingly, Jim moved the conversation on to other things before they parted. Watching him striding, Anne Marie thought, *to look at him, you wouldn't think there was a bother on him.*

Anne Marie walked slowly home, thinking, *here am I wrapped up in myself when there's someone next door; I haven't looked near in a*

week, facing major surgery and smiling, sharing it with me. I don't appreci-
ate how well off I am. People are like hands in many ways, one cleansing
the other.

The house was quiet. Her son and daughter were busy working at home on their computers. Making her way to the kitchen,
rucksack in hand, she passed Bert's study. The door was open.
It was always open now. She could see him, in his swivel chair,
chewing on the end of an unlit pipe, nose in a book. All he said
when told she had given up smoking was, "I'm proud of you."

The two years had flown by since he passed. Anne Marie
missed him. Often consoling herself with the thought that it
wasn't Covid-19 that took him, thankful they could part with
dignity.

She made herself busy preparing the evening meal. It would
be ready and waiting for her children when they logged off and
finished work for the day. White slavery, on-call 24/7, she often
thought. It's a different world for them, alright—no doubt about
that.

Over dinner, they chatted about their day. Her son and
daughter, both IT engineers, used language she didn't understand when talking to each other. Anne Marie, for her part, told
them about her walk and, without going into detail, some of the
people she had met. She did laughing, tell-all about the incident
in the supermarket and the old lady who came to her rescue,
while at the same time making a mental note to repay her generosity tomorrow. She thought about telling them about Jim but
couldn't bring herself to do it. It could wait until tomorrow.

After checking the doors, turning off the kitchen lights at
nine o'clock, content the house was secure, Anne Marie, plead-
ing tiredness, said goodnight and went to her bedroom. She was
tired, but she knew sleep wouldn't come easily. Kneeling by her
bedside, missal and other prayer aids to hand, Anne Marie

worked through her formulaic litany of prayers and, feeling empty, repeated the process. Nothing happened. She wasn't connecting. When she tried to give up smoking, she prayed. Her prayers didn't stop her smoking. Confiding her disappointment to Bert, he just laughed, saying, "What did you expect? God to intervene? You'll stop when you want to."

Good old pragmatic Bert. He was right, she conceded.

Suddenly she was two years back in time, sat at Bert's hospital bed, holding his hand through the long night, ferociously asking God to intercede on his behalf. Anne Marie, through her tears, made all sorts of promises praying for Bert's recovery. Morning sunlight was brightening the gloomy ward when Bert died. Left with nothing to do, she petitioned God for Bert's salvation.

Slowly she prised herself up off her knees unfulfilled, opened the window blinds, switched off the room lights, and stood gazing into the blackness of the night. Her mouth was dry, mind blank; she felt lifeless. Anne Marie was so tired she had hardly the energy left to get herself into bed. She lay on the side of the bed she always lay on when Bert was with her. Putting herself beside the hollow he made in the memory mattress comforted her. She tried praying again. Unable to focus, she tossed one way, then the other squirming in feelings of dubiety, wondering if she could ever pray again.

In desperation, Anne Marie sat up, opened a pack of cigarettes, extracted one, put it in her mouth, found her lighter, paused before she set the lighter aside, removed the cigarette from her mouth and put it back in its pack. Breathing a deep sigh, Anne Marie settled back down into her bed.

Slowly, unencumbered, she began praying again, silently forming images and concepts in her mind. She pondered The Sermon on the Mount, particularly the Beatitudes, against the backcloth of her encounters with the people she had met on her morning walk. It was a thorough examination of conscience that revealed her poverty of spirit. *I can't see things the way You see them. I view my world through a different set of lenses. How many times did I meet You today, and did I recognise You?* Anne Marie thought about and prayed for all the people she met and talked to during the day, especially Jim coping with cancer and Cecil with muffled hearing. In closing, she promised to try harder to embrace the challenges of the Beatitudes. To do that, Anne Marie knew she would need the God within to open her heart wider.

As sleep overwhelmed her, Anne Marie heard Bert whispering, "You'll see clearer tomorrow, Anne Marie if you wear your glasses."

Anne Marie fell asleep laughing.

A Very Ordinary Spy

Alfie is sitting downstairs in the front room of a lacklustre two-storey terrace house in Albert Street. His mother pretentiously labelled it - the parlour, into which she fussily ushered the occasional visitor. Few ever made it beyond the parlour.

Alfie was born in this house a lifetime ago. Apart from the new kitchen, bathroom and central heating, it hasn't changed much. Sat, cramped in his chair, at a small table, angled in front of a narrow sliding sash window, Alfie can see the string of Mill Brae terraced houses, stepping pedantically upwards out of sight.

It's busier now with vehicles than it was back then. An occasional stooping pedestrian plods wearily up the Brae. In former times, beyond the summit was farmland. Now, the arable land and the golf course have yielded to unimpressive housing estates. Up and over the Brae was a favourite playground for children, disappearing like pioneers into a vast, welcoming expanse of unexplored wilderness.

Panning right, twisting his neck, a herd of Friesian cows, released from morning milking, grazed contentedly in Magill's front field. Alfie could see further to the right in his mind's eye, the Grammar School sheltering behind a shield of hawthorn hedging. The intersection where Cairncastle Road joins Albert Street, Meetinghouse Street, Church Lane and Mill Brae is also in plain view. Alfie knows this neighbourhood, this area, its secret places.

Alfie features in this story, but it's not about him. It's about someone he knew very well. They grew up together in the labyrinth of streets, lanes, and alleys that bind this neighbourhood. Alfie cannot tell you his name because they parted a long time ago. Alfie calls him Dave.

Dave, born and reared on the Mill Brae, eagerly took to schooling. He won against the run of play; some might say, a much-prized scholarship. It was the only scholarship awarded that year to the local grammar school just over the road from where he lived. Dave, oblivious to the fact he was the only non-fee paying student, escorted by his mother, walked suitably uniformed the short distance from the Mill Brae, up the Cairncastle Road, to his new school, into his future. He settled quickly, a world of imagination and possibility unfolding. His only discomfort was the irritating itch; he suffered wearing the school uniform. It was something that set him apart, he felt, from his pals, only reunited when he ran home, hurriedly discarding the uniform, to be with them doing things they always did around the neighbourhood.

It wasn't all plain sailing for Dave, a scholarship boy, in a grammar school. He sensed that some fellow students felt he shouldn't be there; he was somehow out of place. They harboured resentment, which at first he couldn't fathom until it dawned on him that he was rooted in very different ground from them. Dave's family, working-class – tradesmen and artisans, theirs middle-class – doctors, lawyers, business people. Reared in the crucible of a big family, he experienced major and minor crises – the ups and downs, successes and failures of everyday life. The youngest in his family, Dave wasn't spoiled, mollycod-dled or privileged in any way. Family life nurtured, readied and furnished him with the means of surviving the vagaries and wimpiness of life. Ignoring the resenters, secure in the knowledge that he had earned his place, Dave quietly, diligently, settled to his studies.

He was one of those annoyingly talented people. Everything seemed easy to him: science, maths, literature, sports, even music which, considering he had never touched a musical instru-ment at home, never banged on a tin drum as a child, was quite remarkable. He tried to explain it to Alfie once, relating musical notation to maths through series, patterns, repetitions and rhythms, scribbling symbols on a scrap of paper. Alfie, better informed, was sadly none the wiser, but Dave was top of his class.

He was good at sports, preferring soccer to rugby, even though he captained the school rugby team. Dave, tall, rangy, and wiry, could play any position, including the front row when needed. Holding his own against any opposition, giving as good as he got on the rugby field, was a challenge he wholeheartedly embraced. Applying himself to his studies, Dave hungrily read everything he could get his hands on and played football with his neighbourhood pals at every opportunity. He was one of the boys.

Towards the end of Dave's second year, an incident per-suaded his classmates to view him through a different prism. His class was in the gym one afternoon for a period of physical ed-ucation. The teacher produced a set of boxing gloves, big spar-ring gloves, tossed a pair to Dave, held up the other gloves and invited anyone who fancied a bit of sparring to don them. A stocky, broad-shouldered front-row forward – a resenter – put on the gloves and squared up to Dave. They circled each other for a moment or two. Losing patience, his opponent lunged at Dave, who nimbly sidestepping patting him on the back of the head as he went past. His opponent did not appreciate Dave's nimble manoeuvre, but on-looking classmates, thinking it funny, laughed. Red-faced, the resenter turned and flew at Dave again, earning himself, this time a pat on the cheek. That tap was like a red rag to a bull—the enraged bull charged at Dave, fists flailing like tattered cloth windmill sails in a gale. Evading the flurry of fists, Dave landed a fierce right-hand punch on his assailant's chin, knocking him flat on his back. The sparring session ended abruptly. Dave's progress through school from that moment proceeded without hindrance.

Dave's transition from school to university was a natural progression, and it was a journey into the unknown no one in his working-class neighbourhood had made before. Dave went to university in England. As a custom and excise officer, Alfie joined the civil service, trained in Dublin Castle, and was posted to Belfast. University shaped Dave's life. Fluent in four languages, competent in others, he could have served in the diplomatic service anywhere in the world. But he was nurtured, and then recruited into the British Secret Service Bureau, MO3. In 1912, Dave, posted in Berlin, was gathering intelligence on events in Germany.

In the United Kingdom, the Third Home Rule Bill was passed by the House of Commons. Home Rule in Ireland, for Ulster Unionists synonymous with Rome Rule, was perceived as a threat to their cultural and national identity, and there was opposition. When allusions surfaced, in the ether of political scheming, on the creation of a force in Ulster to fight against the imposition of Home Rule in Ireland, the Secret Service Bureau trawled its establishment in search of an agent, to put on the ground, to gather intelligence.

A civil servant posted to Belfast, living with his parents in Albert Street, Alfie had the freedom to travel, wherever his work took him. Over time, deep-seated societal differences concerning the home rule issue became self-evident. Unionists were uneasy, apprehensive and opposed to it. Alfie reported what he discerned to his superiors. He had to. It was his duty.

Dave, well informed of affairs in Germany, always spent his annual leave at home with his parents. Alfie could see Dave's house through the window. Very well known locally, respected, popular, one of the boys, an Ulster-Scots natural speaker, when occasion demanded it, in his natural habitat, Dave seamlessly blended in. MO3 needed an agent with an authentic background cover. Dave was in every respect that agent; he could be himself; a very ordinary spy. Alfie, because they were friends, became his handler.

In the summer of 1912, Dave was home as usual on six weeks annual leave – the last two weeks in June and the month of July. Except, it wasn't as usual for Dave; he was on an intelligence-gathering mission for MO3 – doing what spies do. His brief was to confirm what Alfie had reported and provide more reliable, in-depth intelligence.

On familiar ground, Dave was himself, meeting up with old mates, visiting old watering holes at weekends, standing at touchlines on Saturdays watching football, and chatting to the folk he met. His ears always attuned listened for anything that would inform his intelligence-gathering mission. He was an excellent listener, ardently British, benignly self-associating. "People talking tell you stuff without knowing it," he would often say. "Listening isn't hard work. Keeping your mouth shut, that's the trick."

Dave confirmed Alfie's reports in his first week home, adding that opposition to home rule was gaining momentum. It was palpable. Society rubbing along in parallel was like lodgers in a boarding house moving in different cultural directions. Dave's reports were concise, without embellishment or analysis. The latter he left to headquarter experts. Convinced, however, that something momentous was brewing, he stalked it relentlessly. Dave was in a world where ordinary people going about their everyday business lost their mantle of ordinariness.

Regularly Dave walked around the harbour area, along the shorefront past the bathing houses, noting anything of interest with his eagle eyes and committing it to memory. By nature and training, Dave was surveillance conscious. It was like acute sensory perception, a sixth sense, an eye in the back of the head. He varied his daily routine, often taking long walks on his own, wandering the townlands of youth, but always alert. Dave never met his handler Alfie secretly or used drop boxes to pass information. Their exchanges were casual, using everyday language, in company with others. If Alfie had pointed Dave in a particular direction, he would find an oblique way of acknowledging its usefulness or otherwise in general conversation,

"You were right about that," he would say about something trivial, knowing Alfie would pick up on it.

On one of his walks along the shorefront, Dave spotted a small fishing boat tying up at a mooring post, midway between the bathing houses. He hadn't noticed the mooring post before or the stone steps down to it from the path above. A man on the boat picked up a box and made his way up the steps to where Dave stood leaning over the railing.

"What are you at the day?" Dave greeted him, inviting conversation.

"I'm away up to the big house with their catch of the day," the man replied, "and I can tell you, it's a bit of a trek up through

96

the trees to get to it," he continued, shifting the box to his other shoulder.

"Never knew boats came in here before?" Dave said, nodding at the mooring post.

"Only wee boats like mine can moor at Smiley's Post when the tide's right and not for long either," the fisherman answered, resting his box of fish on the railing.

"That's a big lot of fish you have there. Do you do this often?"

"Auch, they're always entertaining someone up in the big house, but this past wee while it has been very busy. I'll need to be going; otherwise, I'll miss the tide and end up high and dry. I'd look a right fool then, wouldn't I?" he said, laughing, heaving the box onto the other shoulder, and making his way over to the plantation of tall trees gracing the Bank Heads.

Dave, watching him plod away, noticed for the first time the winding trail up through the trees to the Smiley home – Drumalis. He had walked past it so many times and hadn't seen it. Small wonder it wasn't a trail; it was little more than a frequently used spoor. Dave hadn't noticed Smiley's mooring post either. But something about Drumalis rang a bell in Dave's mind. He couldn't pin it down. It lingered. The big house, always entertaining, busier than usual! Was there a connection?

Dave walking on, pondering the connections, made his way home down the Old Glenarm Road. He decided on impulse to look around the McGarel Cemetery – maybe the open gate was the invitation. Seeing a man pruning shrubs, the connection clicked. The gardener! He had heard, somewhere, something – a gardener employed at Drumalis – had said about the goings-on up at the big house. The goings-on, it turned out, was more than the usual entertaining; it was about meetings, influential people, business meetings. But what kind of business? It was a thread needing teasing.

In the weeks that followed, Dave walked past the various entrances to Drumalis and saw only an occasional motor vehicle entering or leaving the estate. Nothing out of the ordinary. One evening walking up Tower Road towards the town centre, he saw three motor vehicles, one after the other, disappear into Drumalis estate through a little-used entrance. It wasn't a lodged entrance, more a farm entrance. When he reached it, the gate was closed, he couldn't see anything. Convinced his scraps of intelligence had merit that something was afoot in Drumalis, Dave furnished his final report at the end of July, his so-called vacation over and told friends he was going back to Germany. His report stated that unionist opposition to home rule was intense, influential people were involved in planning something to oppose the imposition of home rule, and the use of arms could not be ruled out.

After debriefing in London, Dave was posted back to Germany.

In Berlin, he learned that Sir Edward Carson had read the Ulster Covenant from the steps of the ancestral home of Sir James Craig on 19th September 1912 and that on the 28th September 1912, over a quarter of a million men, led by Carson, signed the Covenant in City Hall Belfast. Dave was aware that some thought the unionist threat of opposing home rule a huge game of brinkmanship, but he has reservations on that score. As the New Year, 1913 dawned, both sides of the home rule issue prepared for armed conflict. The House of Lord's rejection of the Home Rule Bill in January 2013 did nothing to dampen unionist opposition to home rule.

Dave, from the faintest of whispers, on butterfly wings, was fully cognizant in January 1913 that persons unknown were sourcing munitions suppliers in Germany. Approaches had been made to arms dealers in Hamburg, Vienna and Milan; Dave was recalled to London, and customs and excise officials seized caches of arms bound for Ireland; Alfie was one of the customs officers.

The foundation of the Ulster Volunteer Force in 1913 added a keener edge to the notion of brinkmanship. Dave returned to Berlin, his antennae searching for other valuable whispers, before returning home on compassionate leave. MO3 needed Dave on the ground gathering intelligence, should action by Government be deemed necessary.

Home on compassionate leave – his mother's deteriorating health the reason, allegedly – his mother didn't know it – plausible cover for a spy. It was immediately apparent to Dave that defiance had superseded unionistic opposition to home rule. It was on everyone's lips, no concealment, ordinary folk ready to fight for the cause. The air was laden with intoxicating expectancy. It was all that men gathered on street corners talked about. In the marketplace on Station Road, seething with shoppers, folk in from the country on a day out, rabid opposers of home rule vented their anger. The town celebrated the 12th of July with added zest; flags flew triumphantly, arches stood defiantly, drums thundered threateningly, bands played rancorously, and orators spoke passionately.

Romania and Turkey invaded Bulgaria. Nobody in this part of Ireland noticed.

The seizure of a large cache of arms in London, bound for Ulster, confirmed Dave's intelligence and much more. The arms purveyor and associates were revealed – the Major and his twelve apostles. Dave convinced that Drumalis was pivotal, patrolled the estate's boundaries. Of particular interest was motor vehicle access. There were six possibilities. He discounted access from Chaine Memorial Road, by way of Bay Road, because it was too long, slow, and public. He eliminated the farm entrance off Tower Road, deeming the track to the house unsuitable for heavy motor vehicles. The entrance from the narrow Bank Heads lane, offering privacy, lost its value with brazen opposition to home rule. That left the three gate lodge access possibilities; Curran Road, Glenarm Road beside the Congregational Church, and Glenarm Road's main entrance opposite Victoria Street.

Access from Glenarm Road beside the Congregational Church close to a busy junction was he thought too public and access from Curran Road through the plantation of elms too laborious. The best access for quick and easy entry and exit was the main entrance on Glenarm Road. That was where Dave focused attention without neglecting the other options. He varied the times and patterns of his reconnaissance walks, acutely searching for deviations in routine behaviour, personal, situational, environmental and social. Any indicator of something untoward.

Dave needed to know when the Major and his apostles met and what precisely they were planning. Logic told him busy men would meet in the evenings and choose occasions when the town was busy. Saturdays, market days, perhaps?

One evening in late July, shortly before seven o'clock, passing the main entrance on Glenarm Road, Dave saw a middle-aged couple, lodge residents he assumed, near the railings tending flower beds. Dave, never foregoing an opportunity to engage in conversation, remarked how neat and tidy their garden looked. Pleased at the compliment, the man stood up, stretching his back, as the woman, presumably his wife, acknowledged Dave saying, "It's not hard to keep in shape if you do a wee bit every day."

As they chatted, a black car slowly drove in, the man Dave had been engaging in conversation raised a forefinger to his cap in deference, and the car proceeded up the broad avenue. Dave didn't look to see who was in the car; the touching of the forelock told him all he needed to know. Three more cars entered in quick succession, each acknowledged by the deferring forefinger, was sufficient confirmation. Having seen enough, Dave didn't linger. He noted that it was the last market day of the month, but he didn't know how frequently the meetings were scheduled and if they were always on market days. Convinced that Drumalis was the nerve centre of home rule opposition, he had to find out what was going on. To do that, Dave had to get closer.

Making his way back down the Bank Heads past Smiley's Post, he leaned against the railings looking up at the grove of tall native trees, sycamore, oak, beech, ash, and horse chestnut, all fully dressed in their summer foliage. Carpets of bluebells and clusters of primrose bedecked the forest floor. The route the fisherman had taken up to the house, almost invisible, Dave could only see because he knew it was there. But he also knew that if he were to take that route, his trail would be visible in Scotland. In any case, there were too many eyes about, the night sky too clear and bright. Beyond the tall majestic trees, the hidden house, out of sight, was unapproachable. It was too risky. He had to find another way.

Dave continued his daily self-associating routines, affably being all things to all people, fitting in. His nocturnal routine was something else. He would, suitably attired, in late afternoons go on long hikes into the countryside. But on the last market day of the month, as evening approached, he would be at the northernmost end of the estate, inside the tree line. His light-coloured reversible jacket would become black. Donning black headgear and gloves, Dave was a silent shadow among the trees and shrubs. Stealthily, stalking his way along the narrow tracks used by estate foresters, he approached the house. Dave's observations enabled him to establish that meetings were scheduled for the last market day in each month. He also confirmed the meetings would be convened in the dining room. But it wasn't enough; Dave needed to know what they were planning. That meant getting close enough to hear what was being said.

Early in October, activity around Drumalis estate increased, making Dave think that the frequency of meetings would also increase. November's darker nights, offering better cover, emboldened Dave. He was in position, hidden in the trees north side of the house for the market day meeting in November. The light from the dining room cast an amber glow over the shrubbery outside. Confident and secure in their surroundings, the assembly set about their business with the window shutters open. Hidden, Dave could see into the dining room; the marble fireplace, the two chandeliers hanging from the ceiling casting shadows around the room, wood-panelled walls filled with paintings and family portraits. In the middle was the mahogany dining table surrounded by high back chairs, in which the twelve apostles sat looking at the Major standing in front of a blackboard mounted on an artist's easel, his back to Dave. As he spoke to the apostles, the Major's shoulders flexed instinctively, easing the burden of command. The black coated, white-shirted apostles, some bearded, one or two moustached, sat upright in attentive bearing. Dave couldn't hear. He had to get closer.

There had been no rain for several days; the ground was firm, crawling slowly, stealthily, noiselessly towards the window nearest the Major, out of the line of sight, below sill level, through the shrubbery, until he was within hearing distance. In position, he froze, scarcely breathing, melting into the shrubbery. Listening to what was being discussed, his pulse rate increased until his heart was pounding his ribcage. It wasn't opposition; it was insurrection. Delivery of vast quantities of arms, already procured, delivery as scheduled, confirmed, was greeted with apostolic applause. Planning meetings would be convened to finalise details on collection and distribution. The meeting ended shortly after ten o'clock. Dave didn't move a muscle until he heard the motor cars driving off. Stiff, sore, cold, and deeply troubled Dave retreated carefully without leaving a trace.

Alfie read Dave's report before forwarding it to London. The scale of what was intended was beyond imagination.

As Christmas neared, activity in Drumalis noticeably slowed. It was to Dave as if the world had paused to catch its breath—a brief respite before the impending storm.

After Christmas, the pace of activity around Drumalis increased. Standing, clad all in black, hands gloved, face blackened, concealed in the trees, in a different vantage point, looking at the unlit dining room windows, Dave heard feet crunching gravel on the path, around the house before he saw them. He froze, slowly nose-breathing deeply in case his exhaled breath gave him away; armed men were patrolling the perimeter of the house. The light switched on in the dining room silhouetted them before the shutters closed the night out. Dave felt a coldness creep across his shoulders and slowly spread down his body into his feet. Hairs on the back of his neck stood in fear. He listened for dogs but didn't hear any. Distribution of the arms was imminent; it was only a matter of when and how. He stood like a rabbit caught in the light of a lamper, afraid to move until reason prevailed. All he could do was retreat, report back and wait.

His report to London was concise as usual – planning for the distribution of large quantities of munitions to be used in armed conflict against the imposition of home rule was proceeding at pace – distribution was imminent – when precisely and how not yet determined –Drumalis nerve centre of operations. Alfie forwarded Dave's report to MO3.

Dave, impatiently waiting for orders, was intent on eavesdropping on the next meeting in Drumalis. Alfie strenuously advised against it, forcefully argued against it, pleaded with him, to no avail.

"It's my duty and I must try," Dave said, brushing Alfie's protestations aside.

Dave's mind firmly set, Alfie had no option but to inform MO3. He had to; it was *his* duty. Alfie hoped MO3 would order Dave to desist.

No counter order arrived and so, Dave went back to Drumalis to eavesdrop on the next meeting, knowing that he would have to tread very carefully and that security around the big house might have been strengthened further with the deployment of an outer perimeter of guards.

That was the last time Alfie saw Dave.

For a while, Dave wasn't missed. Friends asked questions, to which the stock in trade answer was – called back to London – thunder clouds gathering over Germany – expertise in that area needed – satisfied their curiosity. His parents would say to themselves – 'not like him to leave without saying' – anxiously waiting for word from him. Alfie, in his heart, knew no word would come from Dave. But he couldn't tell Dave's parents that. Could he?

Smuggled munitions landed at Larne Harbour on Friday and Saturday the 24th and 25th April 2014 were transported into

Drumalis through the Curran Road gate entrance to avoid embarrassing the local constabulary and distributed out the main Glenarm Road entrance to all over Ulster.

Declaration of World War 1 in August that year put the home rule issue on hold, leaving both sides of the impasse to fight a common enemy on foreign soil.

Months after the start of the war with Germany, Dave's parents did get word – a telegram from the War Office – missing on active service presumed dead.

On his last foray into Drumalis, Alfie believed that Dave was captured and taken prisoner. Only Alfie and MO3 knew that Dave was going to Drumalis that night – no one else. There was no order from MO3 for Dave to desist. Not by nature a risk-taker; Dave was cautious. His captors would have persuaded him by whatever means to reveal all. No doubt Dave told them he was ardently British, serving His Majesty, a loyalist, doing his duty. It would have fallen on deaf ears. Dave died in the line of duty, Alfie believed. Some would say murdered.

Alfie often wondered if they buried Dave somewhere on the estate; there were ample burial places in Drumalis Estate. Walking his dog, Alfie inexpertly searched for any disturbed ground but found none. The disposal of Dave's body could have been at sea, bagged and taken down to Smiley's Post, loaded onto a boat, weighted and dropped overboard, somewhere out at the Maidens lighthouse, in the dead of night, never to be found.

Alfie's thoughts often returned to the fisherman Dave met at Smiley's Post. Was that meeting happenstance? In many walks past it at high tide, Alfie never saw a boat moored at Smiley's Post and not without the want of trying ever encountered anyone who had. The way to Drumalis House, through the trees on the Bank Heads, the fisherman used, didn't tempt Dave. Alfie knew that.

*

Twenty years after Dave went missing, in the auction room at the foot of Saint Johns Place, Alfie was plundering boxes of bric-a-brac, as he often did in search of a surprise. Alfie's speculative bid on a nice looking lot secured it for little money. In the shed in his back yard, picking through the pile of stuff emptied onto the bench, Alfie found a watch. It wasn't the dull gold that caught his eye, but the moment he saw it, Alfie knew it was Dave's. His hand trembled, picking it up. Dave's treasured item was the watch his parents gave him when he went off to university. The inscription on the back told all.

Boys swinging on a rope looped around the branch of a big oak tree in the plantation opposite Smiley's Post had recently unearthed it, scraping their feet on the ground as they swung to and fro.

Alfie still has the watch, and his son thinks it's going to be his. Someday it will, but will Alfie tell his son its history? Maybe.

If you are about Drumalis on a January evening, don't be alarmed if you encounter a tall and rangy, wiry young man dressed in black.

Dave has been sighted on the north side of Drumalis many times.

He was a very ordinary spy.

Author's Note: This story is inspired by a document found in a black leather pouch wedged between the rafters and slated roof of a house on Albert Street, Larne, Co. Antrim, Northern Ireland in the 1980s. The document initialled *A Mc K* sheds new light on events over a century ago.

An Encounter with a Mermaid

Mary Louise, a teenager, was helping her father clear out the attic of their home. All of the stuff in it was her great grandfather's; most of it, of little monetary value, destined for the recycling centre. Mary Louise liked pottering around with old things. Everything had a history, and for something that hadn't, she enjoyed inventing one. History was her passion.

It was late Saturday afternoon when Mary Louise, job done, left the attic carrying a small box full of what looked like jumble. She set it aside to rummage after she had rid herself of attic dust and grime. Showered, feeling clean, she emptied the box onto the big kitchen table. All sorts of bits and pieces and odds and sods awaited her discerning eye: a cut-throat razor, a wad of foul-smelling tobacco, a bunch of keys and much more.

One eye-catching item was a small leather-bound pocket-book tied in a bow with a bright red ribbon. It was the first thing Mary Louise picked up. Five inches wide and seven inches long, it fitted neatly into the palm of her hand. Ribbon undone, she carefully opened the book. Inside it, she found a neatly folded nineteenth-century ordnance survey map of her home town annotated in her great grandfather's hand. Curiosity aroused Mary

Louise settled down to read. Little did she know she was embarking on a journey of discovery.

Mary Louise, now firmly set in the nineteenth century, continued her journey of discovery on Sunday afternoon, walking the route her great grandfather had annotated. Her home, a substantial three-storey terraced townhouse on the left side of Curran Road, was at one time her great grandfather's. In the 1800s, Curran Road was called Curran Street. The other side of the street, the sea side, was virgin grassland. Buildings, including the Orange Lodge and churches, yet to be built.

Nearing the Tower Road junction, two terraces of two-story parlour fronted houses stood proudly on either side of the impressive gated entrance to Drumalis Estate. The serpentine cast iron railings that today frame Corran Manor Road, Mary Louise noted, was all that remained of the Drumalis Estate gated entrance from Curran road. Referring again to her map she can see on Tower Road, substantial detached townhouses with extensive gardens and entrances leisurely stretch up over the hill and gently glide down towards the sea. An eight-foot-high granite stone wall on the opposite side of the road bounds Drumalis Estate. Big detached townhouses, with gardens front and rear, enjoyed unobstructed sea views along Chaine Memorial Road. Merchants, mariners, industrialists, people of substance, position, status and influence resided there.

A picturesque cottage on a corner plot at Bay Road junction is eye-catching, and it is not an anachronism. Still perfectly functional, it was, of its time, the first dwelling built on what today is known as Chaine Memorial Road as a summer residence for a Belfast industrialist in 1870.

Mary Louise couldn't journey much further along the present Chaine Memorial Road beyond Bay Road because the thoroughfare that once stretched through the Port of Larne connecting with Olderfleet Road is no longer accessible. In her great grand-father's day, a narrow-gauge railway transported limestone, on manually propelled bogies, from a quarry at Waterloo Bay, past the cottage, into Larne Harbour for shipment abroad. As Larne Harbour, led by Mr Chaine, rapidly developed, limestone quarrying at Waterloo Bay declined. After he died in 1885, a memorial round tower was built in 1887 at Sandy Bay Point. To facilitate its construction, a road to Sandy Bay Point, from the north pier of Larne Harbour, was needed to transport the heavy granite building blocks. That road past the cottage to Sandy Bay Point, replacing the narrow-gauge railway, was the beginnings of the Chaine Memorial Road.

Standing in front of the cottage, notebook in hand, it was difficult for Mary Louise to imagine that once there were substantial gardens around the dwelling through which peacocks proudly strutted. That's what her great grandfather had written in his notebook. Facing down Bay Road towards Curran Road, detached garden fronted dwellings yield to semi-detached to terraced gardened fronted houses. One's place in Victorian society there for all to witness.

At Bay Road and Curran Road junction, Sea View House, now a guest house, leans towards the Harbour Road; red brick panelled walled in on one side by the former Aluminium Works buildings and the other by railway tracks. Her great grandfather's notes tell of families on their way to the Islandmagee ferry, for a day picnicking on the island, happily walking down that road, children by their sides, buckets and spades in hand.

Folk would gather at the edge of the pier, particularly at weekends, to watch the Stranraer boat docking. It was an event. People, people watching to see who was disembarking; *it must have been something special then,* she thought. She read about boys too, sitting, legs dangling over the edge of the piers, hopefully fishing.

With public access denied through the harbour from Chaine Memorial Road and the Harbour Road now closed too, she couldn't follow in the footsteps of her great grandfather. But there was somewhere she had to go. Fleet Street is a narrow street with a history of its own. At the harbour end of Fleet Street, access to the left is only for those travelling by sea or train. To the right stretches Olderfleet Road. In former times, her notes tell her, it was possible to walk through the harbour from Chaine Memorial Road to Olderfleet Road. But the roots of the story in Mary Louise's notebook predate the construction of those roads.

A vacant plot at Fleet Street and Olderfleet Road junction denotes where the Olderfleet Hotel once stood. It opened for business in 1878, providing much-needed accommodation for travellers and the growing tourism trade.

The hotel stood three stories, overlooking Larne Lough, with unobstructed views of Islandmagee, over which the morning sun rose. It was a substantial Victorian building in every respect, externally and internally. Bow windows rose from the ground floor to the roof of the front facade. From 'The Prom', access to the hotel was by a set of elegant tiled steps onto an expansive terrace that stretched the length of the building. The entrance to the hotel was generously wide. Above the magnificent mahogany doors, a stained glass semi-circular fanlight illuminated the way into a vast foyer furnished with Victorian flamboyance. The polished floors gleamed, the windows were hung with rich floor–to–ceiling coloured drapes, cushioned seating with little side tables sat in expectation of service and at the end of the foyer, an ornate fireplace housing a grate readied for use when needed. Everything was colour coordinated to create a harmonious ambience. The hotel is long gone, but from her great grandfather's notes, Mary Louise knew about the two Victorian terraces of three-storey townhouses on Olderfleet Road.

The Royal and Bellevue Terraces were built, long before the Olderfleet Road was made, facing '*The Prom*', a narrow track surfaced with packed gravel and stretching past the Olderfleet Castle, serving the shipbuilding yards located out at Curran Point. It was protected on its seaward side by a five-foot-high granite stone retaining wall against which Larne Lough ebbed and flowed until reclaimed for the development of the Port of Larne in the twentieth century.

Mary Louise clutching the notebook, hurried along Olderfleet Road to view the terraces, excitement mounting in her breast. She was enjoying the search. Walking close to the dwellings, her initial excitement withered. There was nothing much to see; they're like the house I live in, she thought. Crossing to the opposite side of the road, she slowly retraced her steps, changing her mind, picking out, as she walked, different delightful features on the terraces' facades. Quirky little turrets, cornices, lantern roof lights above the bow windows and windows half-hidden below ground level caught her searching eye. She figured that the terraces had basements. Her home didn't have a basement. For a moment, she felt envious. Walking with renewed intent, her eyes lasering in, she noticed that not all of the houses in the terraces were the same. Modern roof lights had replaced period lantern roof lights, and chimneys had been removed, resulting in loss of character for some. Others cried out to her to come and have a closer look. Mary Louise wanted to sprint across the road, but she curbed her rising excitement and walked briskly across, camera and notebook in hand, as ladylike as she could manage.

She stood unashamedly gawking through a window into what she took to be a sitting room. Everything was in order; nothing was out of place. Every surface, table, sideboard, mantelpiece and wall was filled with things that screamed Victorian at her. She was tempted to ask for a guided tour but contented herself looking in. Front entrances were framed with majestic fluted capped and corniced columns with tall cast iron lampstands on either side. In one house, a crystal chandelier bore silent witness. Front gardens filled almost to overflowing with colourful figurines and sculptures screamed Victoriana to passers-by. These are museums of the Victorian lifestyle, she thought. Her mother would have said, 'too much clutter, dear'. There was nothing minimalistic about the Victorians. Then she thought, *where did all my great grandfather's stuff go?* She'd never know, not that it mattered much. Thanks to his notes, Mary Louise had acquired an appreciation of Victorian architecture, interior design, and taste.

Standing her back to the terraces reading her great grandfather's notes, she wondered what it must have been like to live in the Victorian era. Her imagination found wings and soared as Larne Lough ebbed and flowed beyond the granite retaining wall protecting '*The Prom*' from the moon's tidal pull. Sailboats moved around tacking the wind, and a wooden jetty like a long tongue, reached out into the Lough to allow larger boats to serve passengers. Folk promenading past her, watched the goings-on as she did. Fishermen about their business and swimmers too added interest for watchers. A hive of summer activity filled her imagination with vivid colours and happy noises.

In her bedroom Mary Louise found a flier promoting the hotel that her great grandfather had kept. The hotel opening for business in 1878 offered something new:

Olderfleet Hotel
First Class Hotel, close to the landing stage of
Stranraer Steamer – The Gateway to
Antrim's Famous Glen and Coastal Scenery.
Convenient to Golf Links
The restful atmosphere of the Hotel and the
Wonderfully invigorating quality of the air
Combine to make this the ideal holiday
Residence.
Hot and Cold Sea Water Baths. Ample
Garage accommodation
– OPEN ALL THE YEAR ROUND –
LARNE HARBOUR
Grams, "Olderfleet Hotel."
Phone: Larne 7

Inlet and outlet pipes from the Lough, controlled by a simple ball cock and a manual operating mechanism, serviced the hotel's seawater baths. The ballcock shut down the inflow when a pre-set seawater level was reached; the outflow was manually controlled. At low tide, the pipes serving the baths were clearly visible. The Olderfleet Hotel, like the Royal and Bellevue Terraces, had a basement; on that, her grandfather's notes were specific. The basement was huge, the entire footprint of the building divided into separate compartments, one of which stretched the length of the building. Turning a page expecting to learn more about the Olderfleet Hotel, she was surprised to discover that her great grandfather had chosen to delve into the myths and legends of the area.

It is well known, he wrote, that Larne and its townlands are rich in myths, legends and the lore of the land.

A High King of Ireland fought a naval battle against a Viking Chief in Larne Lough in 1014, and Viking skeleton remains were found along the Lough's shore. Mermaids frequently spotted by fishermen off the coast of Islandmagee drew large crowds to Portmuck, hoping for a sighting. It was said that they took the form of a beautiful woman with the features and complexion of a European. Often they were seen sitting on rocks along the coast of Rathlin Island, drying and combing their long hair. Occasionally mermaids netted by fishermen formed affections, married and raised families. It is believed that mermaids frequent underwater caves to relax and rest. Beneath Dunluce Castle, there is a mermaid's cave, and people go there to be at one with the mermaids. 'I know people who have been there,' he wrote, 'they said, it was a special place.'

With the turn of a page, her great grandfather had rewound the clock centuries. It was as if he was speaking directly to her. *Was this little book waiting in the attic to be discovered by me?* She wondered. The hair on the back of her neck stood on end, and goosebumps formed too. She hesitated, but curiosity compelled her to read on.

A long time ago, a young man, the son of the King of Munster, fled his home with his family to escape the seductive advances of his stepmother. Eventually, they settled in Ulster. A massive eruption occurred, releasing waters from a vast underground lagoon that flooded the land, forming Lough Neagh. The King, his wife, two sons and daughter drowned in the lough, but his teenage daughter survived. Her name was LiBan. Under the floodwater, she found refuge in a cave for a year before morphological transformation occurred; she was reborn as a salmon and then became a mermaid, free to swim the oceans for three hundred years, singing her songs to those with ears to hear.

Her great grandfather's notes continued.

In the sixth century, Saint Comgall visited Magheramorne, his birthplace, with a fellow monk called Beoan. Beoan liked to fish, but the fishing in the Lough and the Glenoe River was poor. Sensing his disappointment, Saint Comgall suggested they try the Larne River. On a bright sunny summer's morning, they sallied forth to fish; moving slowly upstream from the river's mouth, casting their nets as they went, without success. Towards midday, they came to an immense pool through which the water flowed slowly. They sat down on the riverbank to eat their bread and cheese lunch.

Stillness had settled around the plum-shaped pool. Red squirrels quietly scampered through the ring of hazelnut trees surrounding it as the sun cast lengthening tree shadows on the water. The birds muted their songs. There was an aura about the place. A ripple disturbed the surface of the calm water, but they didn't notice it. The rippling continued, agitating the water, attracting their attention.

"It's a fish," Saint Comgall said, rising to his feet.

"A big fish," Beoan responded.

Standing on the riverbank, keeping his shadow off the water, Beoan waited to launch his net. A disturbance in the water was close enough for him to cast with confidence. He felt the net bulge and pull away but held tight. Comgall rushed to his aid. The fish was big. Furiously it fought against capture, threshing and twisting, trying to disentangle itself from the net. It was a fiercely strong fish. Two hours and more it fought for its freedom before they landed it. Comgall and Beoan lay on the riverbank, exhausted, catching their breath, before turning their attention to their catch lying nearby.

They could only see the tail of the fish; it was huge.

"I think it's a salmon," Beoan muttered,

"A mighty big salmon by the look of it," Comgall concurred.

The fish, lying drooped over a small mound, had a huge tail. Its skin wasn't scaly; it was smoother, lighter in colour, and more flesh-like. Standing over the fish, they saw its naked torso and a dark mane spread on either side of it. Astonished, it was some moments before they realised they had netted a mermaid.

Slowly, gently, they eased off the tail, exposing her lower limbs forming. They let her rest without further disturbance until her transformation from mermaid to a human being was complete. As she rose to stand before them, Comgall covered her nakedness with his cloak. Standing unafraid before them, they saw a beautiful fair-skinned teenage girl, looking at them with bright, piercing clear blue eyes and long dark hair caressing her shoulders.

Comgall and Beoan, momentarily lost for words, begged forgiveness for unceremoniously dragging her out of her water world. Firmly she allayed their concerns, telling them that she wanted to be, needed to be taken.

"But you fought so hard to free yourself," Beoan said,

"It was not me; it was the salmon in me that fought you," she replied.

LiBan sat them down by the river bank and told them her story.

"If you had not taken me today, my three hundred years of tenure would have ceased. Now, if I wish, I can have another three hundred years to travel the oceans of the world."

"What if you do not wish it?" Saint Comgall asked.

"I will die," LiBan answered.

"You chose death?" Saint Comgall probed.

"I choose martyrdom; I want to be with my creator forever. That's all I want. I have not been baptised; will you baptise me, please, Sir, then I will be free forever."

On the 23rd of July, by the banks of the Larne River, Saint Comgall baptised LiBan, bestowing on her the name Muirgen, meaning born of the sea. Then they made haste to Comgall's monastery before the new day dawned. Surrounded by a community of chanting monks, LiBan passed into eternal life.

Muirgen, Mary Louise was later to learn, is among those listed in the 'Lives of Irish Saints' and is venerated on the 27th January. Her resting place is in the burial ground in an old ruined church in Killeshin, in Donegal.

Then Mary Louise's grandfather's notes added another twist.

Edward Dawson and his teenage daughter alighted from the train at Larne Harbour and walked the short distance to the Olderfleet Hotel. It was Monday the 19th of July 1898, and porters saw to their luggage. At the front desk in the lobby, as Edward completed the registration formalities for their short stay, his daughter, Meriel Liese, sheltered behind him, hiding like a child. She was dressed in a long cotton short-sleeved dress for summer, buttoned at the neck and matching white sandals. Meriel Liese's shoulder-length blond hair was loosely tied behind her head. She was a beautiful, tall teenage girl with an unpretentious open face. Her blue eyes were not deep blue, not clear blue; they were dull, cloudy, sad blue, timid eyes.

Glancing furtively around the lobby while her father busied himself at the reception desk, Meriel Liese watched through the bow window, the red sail of a boat as it slid past. Curiosity piqued, she wandered over to look. Outside, there were colour, noise, activity, and people enjoying the holiday atmosphere on and off the water. Her dull eyes brightened momentarily, and a flicker of delight lightened her face. Her father joined her at the window,

"Shall we take a stroll after we rest and freshen up," he asked.

Meriel Liese smiled her acknowledgement as they made their way to their adjoining rooms on the second floor, where their portered baggage awaited them.

Edward quickly unpacked and, feeling tired, lay down on his bed to rest. Through the open adjoining door, he saw Meriel Liese listlessly remove her clothes piece by piece from her baggage and hang them in the wardrobe, placing smaller items in the chest of drawers. On the bedside table, she carefully positioned a framed photograph of her mother. She glided around the room like a ballerina performing a slow dance; her father, deep in thought, watched.

Meriel Liese's mother, Muriel, had passed away eighteen months earlier, after a long illness that insidiously started when she experienced occasional bouts of tiredness. When her condition worsened, Edward consulted the family doctor; his prescribed treatments failed to remedy her situation. Distraught, Edward sought the best medical advice from near and far. Specialists, even after she had endured a barrage of tests, were unable to arrest her decline. Muriel nursed at home, lost her appetite and slowly wasted away. It was a particularly harrowing duty for Meriel Liese.

Edward grieved Muriel's passing deeply too, but he had seen death before; it was, after all, he knew, the invisible companion that walked the road with every living thing. His teenage daughter's encounter with death was very different; it was her first, and she was deeply wounded. Her mother's death was appalling to witness. Meriel Liese retreated into herself, hiding like someone afraid of the dark, listlessly living without purpose. She was their only child, and Edward worried about her. He hoped that she had not contracted the same wasting illness that her mother had. *Was it hereditary?* He didn't know but was reluctant to subject her to the battery of consultations with physicians and tests, including the psychological probing that would follow to find out if she was only battling grief. He knew he had to be patient.

During Muriel's long illness, physicians, friends, and others obliquely mentioned the Olderfleet Hotel's saltwater baths. Merely hinted, no more than that. The sentiment was that saltwater immersion might offer Muriel some relief, even if only temporarily. Edward hadn't seriously considered their implicit nudges. Muriel, at the time, was too ill to travel from Leitrim, and he couldn't see how immersion in saltwater would benefit her, besides which, he didn't believe in miracles. Later mulling it over, Edward thought it might be worth trying to see if saltwater baths could ease Meriel Liese out of the doldrums that beset her.

He settled his mind and booked into the Olderfleet Hotel for what he hoped would be a week of rest and renewal. Meriel Liese, still unpacking, moved around her room like a shadow; her father sensed the emptiness in her, wondering why he couldn't fill it. *What do you see in your windows of memory Meriel Liese?* he asked himself. *Do you speak your mother's name, loudly to yourself, when I'm not there or quietly to yourself when I'm with you? I fear you have lost the rainbow colours that brightened your rainy days. Is it all dreamlike, snowflakey petal fragments of memory floating in a gossamer bubble? What do you see from within that I cannot see from without? Why do you whimper in your sleep to awaken with redness colouring your eyes?* Edward closed his eyes in silent prayer.

Meriel Liese finished unpacking, stood framed in the connecting door looking down at him when Edward's eyes opened. In the soft afternoon light, she was the image of her mother; his heart leapt for joy. She had tasted bitter tears of sorrow, and somehow he had to fill the void in her life with enabling, liberating love. His problem was he didn't know how to do it. Muriel

119

was the expressive one in their relationship. Refreshed, they left the room to take the air along The Prom.

Outside folk were mingling. It was noisy, colourful, bric-a-brac stalls attracted the curious, and there was a holiday atmosphere about the place. Passing the Olderfleet Castle, Edward shared what little he knew of its history. Beyond the castle, two vessels were taking shape in the shipbuilding yards. From the tip of Curran Point, they stood and looked into the upper reaches of the Lough beyond Glynn and Magheramorne. The sun that had risen over Islandmagee was beginning to settle behind the Inver Braes. It cast a warm evening glow as they strolled back to the hotel in good time for dinner.

They were seated at a table for two, offering a partial view, through a bow window over the lough. Edward sat with his back to the window giving Meriel Liese the view outside, hoping she would sense the relaxed dining room ambience that nevertheless bustled with service activity. Meriel Liese, he noticed, occasionally, shyly, apologetically, searched the room with glances. It was new to them; they didn't know anybody. There were small and large groups of guests, some from observation familiar with the setting, others not. Some formally dressed for dinner, others smart casual attired. Over coffee, he mentioned the seawater baths, one of the hotel's featured attractions, suggesting it might be fun to try. Meriel Liese wasn't keen; he didn't pursue it, letting his good companion patience reign.

It was past nine o'clock when they left the dining room, readying itself for the second sitting and made their way up the dadoe'd ornate staircase to their rooms. Tomorrow, they had a full day's excursion, exploring the Glens of Antrim, departing immediately after breakfast. Meriel Liese, feeling and looking a little tired, kissed her father gently on the cheek, excused herself, closed the connecting door and retired for the night. For a moment, Edward felt deserted, abandoned. Thrusting the unwelcome feelings away, he decided that the best thing to do in the circumstances was to sample the seawater bath. At least it would give him something to relate to Meriel Liese, and if he showed enthusiasm, persuade her to try it.

Dressing gowned, feet slippered, rolled towel clasped under his arm, he headed down the back stairs to find the seawater bath. It was not difficult to find. Pushing in through the magnificent obscure glazed, mahogany double doors, Edward halted. He had expected a tub of sorts, not a swimming pool. He looked around in amazement. The pool, the entire length of the hotel, at least twenty yards wide, was empty. Two-foot square decorative terrazzo tiles covered the floor. Walls were tiled floor to ceiling with glossy deep green tiles that shimmered in the amber glow of the upward-facing stylish new electric lighting distributed around the pool. Shadows, shaped by imperceptible movements on the pool water surface, danced an elaborate choreography on the shimmering walls, gradually climbing to feature on the richly decorated high ceiling. Monastic feelings of hospitality, tranquillity and seclusion enveloped Edward, immediately putting him at ease.

Disrobed, he gingerly put his toe in the water. It wasn't as cold as he expected. That was something he would happily tell his daughter. Pushing off from the side of the pool, he stretched into a leisurely breaststroke and swam contentedly away. Lost in thought, he hadn't noticed until he paused for a rest that someone else was in the pool. The newcomer, some distance away, seemed to glide effortlessly over the water and at other times forcefully thrust through it, creating a bow wave. Edward continued leisurely swimming until he tired. He was towelling himself dry and robing beside the pool when he caught better sight

of the other swimmer. It was the mane of long black hair streaming out behind that attracted Edward's eye. Watching closely, it
slowly dawned on him that his companion all evening in the
pool was a woman. Smiling, he thought no more about it, left
the pool and made his way back to his room. Standing on his
balcony, he gazed for a while at the sickle-shaped moon, hanging
by a thread, it seemed over his head. Inside curtains drawn, relaxed, refreshed, contented, he read a little before inviting sleep.

Tuesday morning dawned bright and beautiful. After breakfast, Meriel Liese and her father joined fellow tourists to tour the
Glens of Antrim. It was a long entertaining, enjoyable, informa-
tive day, during which a very knowledgeable tour guide illuminated insights into other worlds past and present. Everyone returned to the hotel in such good spirits that many led by their
tour guide joined in over-enthusiastically singing, 'The Green
Glens of Antrim.' Edward, tired but relaxed, sensed Meriel Liese
beside him, letting her inner self ease slightly.

After dinner, through which they reviewed all they had seen
and done on their tour, Edward hinted that a seawater bath
might be a good way of relaxing before bed. He assured Meriel
Liese that the water wasn't as cold as he had expected, choosing
not to describe the pool or the atmosphere because he wanted
it to be a surprise if and when she decided to join him. Edward
was at a loss how to persuade, coax, or re-energise Meriel Liese.
But one thing he had to guard against was being overzealous.
That would be disastrous. Edward, for some reason, chose not
to mention the woman swimmer. When he finished speaking,
Meriel Liese raised her head and looked at him. Her vacant look
answered him.

Upstairs she bid Edward goodnight and slowly closed the
connecting door behind her. Edward stood non-plussed, trying
to find his bearings, trawling his feelings in the cradle of his

heart. Fatherly love eased his mind into fluency; gentle persuasion, he reasoned, is the only oil that will unlock his daughter's grief if that is what ails her.

Refreshed in mind and spirit, Edward made his way down to the seawater pool. Looking forward to it, he was invigorated. It was as if the burden of love was easing if love could ever be a burden. Standing in front of the doors, he paused, gathered himself, took a deep breath, pushed open the doors and walked in. It was a sublime moment of entry into a sanctuary of perfect stillness that was waiting just for him. Inside, the silence deepened; there was piano music playing in his head. Chopin's Etude Op10 No.3. It had rooted in his memory from the first time he heard Muriel play it. It was addictively hypnotic. Edward felt he had entered a temple of listening. He was in a presence. She was with him; he knew that, but there was something more. Gazing into the still water, Edward sensed the depth of the surrounding silence.

Edward, without hesitation, entered the water. It felt warmer, invitingly warmer. He leisurely pushed away from the poolside, breaststroking the buoyant seawater on his first length up the pool. It took several lengths in the serene pool for his mind to reset after the mirage of musings that had flooded it. Suddenly he sensed her presence. He didn't need to look; he just knew she was in the pool, closing in on him. She glided up alongside and passed him with graceful ease. Edward continued breaststroking. The next time she approached him, it was with purpose. The music of the turbulent water alerted him. She surged past so fast that he was sucked forward in her slipstream, but his forward motion slowed as she moved quickly away. Three times with increasing energy and intensity, she surged past him, sucking him forward, faster and further. When Edward reached the far end of the pool, the water lost its energy and calmed. He turned and swam back.

Waiting for him was a beautiful young woman, much younger than he had thought. At that moment, Edward felt that he was a stranger in his own life. He was outside looking in, listening. Inexplicably in deep conversation with this young woman, a stranger he had never met, Edward emptied his store of anxieties about Meriel Liese, opening his heart, pouring out his desperation. Without prompting, he told her how long they would be staying in the hotel, why they were there, and his failure to persuade Meriel Liese to join him in the pool.

She listened until he finished talking, then told him, looking into his eyes, not to worry; his daughter would come to the pool. She was sure of it. His daughter just needed a little more time. Then she swam away. Bemused, Edward swam after her, but he was too slow. When he reached the end of the pool, she was gone.

In his room, Edward wondered if he had imagined the whole encounter. It was so real, so vivid, the young woman so alive. He sometimes had weird dreams. Was that one of them? No, he convinced himself, my imagination can't fly that high, not that sky-high. Tomorrow will be a day of different colours. Sleep on it, he thought. I might have got too much sun today.

Sleep didn't come easy to Edward. He tossed and turned, wrestling with thoughts he didn't want to confront. He gave up trying to sleep. He tried reading a book, but it was hopeless; he couldn't focus. The thought of his daughter grappling with the turbulence of teenage years, caring for and nursing her dying mother, tested his parental skills to the limit. In her sadness, she was little by little withdrawing into herself. He didn't know how to reach her. Or was it more than that? Did the illness that took her mother desire her too? Eventually, sleep overwhelmed him.

Wednesday dawned bright and beautiful, with Edward and Meriel Liese among the early comers for breakfast they could choose their table. Aware that he and Meriel Liese hadn't gotten to know many of their fellow guests yet and thinking that perhaps he was being too protective, he chose a table set for four in one of the bow windows, tempting company. The silky full tide caressed the retaining stone wall. Fishermen were about their business, stallholders arranging their merchandise hoping to tempt the eyes of souvenir hunters and multi-coloured sails filling in a gentle breeze, pushed boats in all directions around the Lough. It was a noisy, chaotic scene full of colour and activity. There was plenty to attract and hold attention.

He hadn't noticed the young woman standing at their table until she said, "May I join you."

Edward, delighted, stood and offered her a seat beside Meriel Liese. Seating rearranged, introductions made, breakfast carried on with the usual exchanges; How long are you staying here? Are you having a good time? What did you do yesterday? Comments exchanged on the menagerie of activity outside and inside interrupted their conversation. *Megan, their breakfast companion is close in age to Meriel,* Edward thought. Observing Meriel Liese and Megan's exchanges, he sensed a change in his daughter's demeanour. Nothing specific. Just a feeling. She was just with someone her age, female to female perhaps. Edward couldn't put his finger on it, but there was something he was sure of that. When Megan turned to ask him something, Edward noticed her porcelain skin with a sprinkle of freckles around her nose, her sea-green eyes and her dark hair tied up in a bun behind her head. For a fleeting moment, he thought he had met her somewhere before, but the moment passed.

Megan, it turned out, was a regular visitor to the area and came every year at this time because she loved the hotel and loved being by the sea. To Meriel Liese, she confided that it had become something of a pilgrimage.

"You must try, while you are here, the invigorating seawater baths, they add minerals from the Dead Sea to the seawater. They're rejuvenating," she advised Meriel Liese.

Edward responded enthusiastically, confessing that he had yet to convince Meriel Liese of their therapeutic benefits.

Megan giving full attention to Meriel Liese started to describe the seawater baths, but Edward apologising, interrupted her, explaining that he hadn't told his daughter anything about the baths because he wanted it to be a big surprise, for if and when she decided to try it for herself. Megan acknowledged Edward and changing tack, expounded on the benefits to health and wellbeing of bathing in seawater infused with Dead Sea minerals, including the therapeutic benefits, such as relaxation, easing of tiredness, muscle soreness and relief for a whole battery of skin conditions. So engaged in conversation were they that they didn't notice the dining room emptying and had to rush to join their excursion. Edward and Meriel Liese were going to the famous Gobbins Cliffs. A must-do, among other things. Megan was meeting up with old friends.

The setting sun lingered over the Inver Braes as Edward and Meriel Liese made their way to the dining room for dinner. Another glorious summers' day's touring to reflect on. Edward this time chose a corner table from which they could appreciate the grandeur and drama in the room; the waiters bustling around servicing, the babbling diner noises, knives and forks scraping on china plates, glasses clinking, the popping of corks, and posers wine tasting. Later a string quartet would entertain as the noises of the day outside yielded to the noises of the night. It was pure hotel dining room theatre, even for the urchins outside looking in before they were like errant pigeons shushed away.

Edward was hoping that the spectacle in the room might help lift his daughter's spirits. However, his primary reason for choosing the table was that he hoped Megan would join them; it offered intimacy. Edward hoped very much that she would. Meriel Liese had mentioned Megan several times during the day; how kind she was, so easy to talk to, and such a good listener.

Edward scanned the room, standing up once for a better view, but Megan was not in the room. He concealed his disappointment. Meriel Liese chatted about how much she enjoyed the day, smiling now and then as she recalled different happenings. Quietly conversing, Edward sensed that she was more alert to what was going on around her and as if on cue, most unlike her, she passed an uncomplimentary remark about a lady sitting across the room from them. Edward merely raised a quizzical eyebrow that made her laugh when she was a child; tonight, she smiled. Inwardly Edward was smiling too. Several times Meriel Liese mentioned Megan, and listening attentively, Edward encouraged his daughter to talk.

Later, he tentatively suggested Meriel Liese take Megan's advice and try the seawater bath, adding that he was sure it was doing him some good. Looking at her father, she concurred, mischievously saying, "You are looking a bit younger."

Edward, shaking his head, responded, "It's not that good. I wish it were!"

The moment between them stretched before Meriel Liese said, 'I'm fatigued, and it's been a long day, perhaps…tomorrow…" leaving what he didn't want to hear unsaid.

But there was hesitation in her voice suggesting the possibility. Edward walked across his room to the adjoining door where his daughter stood framed, took her hands, kissed them, saying, "I love you."

"I know you do!" Meriel Liese assured, "See you in the morning; God Bless, goodnight Father." Slowly easing back into her room, she gently closed the door.

Edward stood staring at the closed door between him and his daughter. It wasn't a partition between them. It was an acknowledged necessity. Even the very best of friends needed their own space sometimes for relationships to flourish. Edward knew that, but he sensed Meriel Liese detaching herself from him a little. Little glimmers of her inner self emerging gave him hope. Contentedly he made ready for the pool. He had looked forward to it all day.

At the doors to the pool, he could feel his heart pounding in his chest. His mind raced back to when he was a child about to enter the confession box to make his first confession. Was he afraid, excited then? He couldn't recall, but how he felt then was similar to how he felt now, stimulated. There was a holiness about the pool, and he wanted to meet the woman again. There was something inexplicable that drew him to her.

Eagerly he thrust the doors open and strode into the pool. It was noisy, discordant; the atmosphere was different. It had lost its mystic, and it wasn't difficult to see why. Family groups were splashing about in the water, having fun. Children were leaping into the water, others throwing balls to one another with gay abandon. Calmness, serenity and order replaced by agitation, the hustle and bustle, disarray and upheaval.

Edward was at first disappointed, displeased, then furious. What are they doing in here? He questioned as if he had the right to ask them when they weren't querying his right to be there. It was his place, his sanctuary; they had no right to muscle in. Feeling dispossessed, cast out, evicted, resentment palpable, Edward wanted it back. He looked around; the woman wasn't there; she wouldn't be, not with all the commotion that was going on. He could have left and returned later when things had settled, but the moment was lost; his stubborn nature shaped his actions; he would not turn away and leave.

Mulishly he plunged into the turbulent water. Refreshingly cold, it cleared his head. Regaining his composure, he started to swim. He would show them. Swimming lengths, avoiding inconsiderate bathers, his temper eased, the anger dissipated. Thwarted, he left disgruntled and went to bed like someone nursing a nasty toothache.

On Thursday morning, entering the dining room, Edward and Meriel Liese saw Megan seated at the table in the bow window where they had sat before. She beckoned for them to join her. It was as if she had been waiting for them. Meriel Liese excitedly exclaimed, "Look, there's Megan," rushing to join her.

Edward willingly followed her lead. It was another glorious morning, with much to see outside and much to talk about over breakfast. At one point, Megan turning to Edward, said, "You've been very quiet. Did you go to the seawater bath last night?"

"Yes, I did," Edward answered as enthusiastically as he could, adding, "It's not to be missed," hoping that Megan would probe no further.

As he spoke, her eyes never left his. She didn't say anything, but Edward nursed a feeling of being thoroughly examined. After breakfast, they again went their separate ways: Megan to visit friends, Edward and Meriel Liese to join another tour. As the day progressed, a hint of spring appeared in Meriel Liese's gait, a lightening in her demeanour with a glimmer of self-assurance. It lifted Edward's heart.

For dinner that evening, Edward chose a different table from where they could discreetly people watch. He scanned the room, knowing that Meriel Liese would be looking for Megan, she wasn't there, but her presence was strong even when out of sight. They talked about the day's activities, occasionally raising their eyes to search the room; still Megan wasn't there. After dinner, they strolled contentedly along The Prom. It was a little while before Edward realised that Meriel Liese had linked her arm in his.

Edward was reluctant to mention the seawater bath; what if his daughter said yes! What if the atmosphere was like last night! Would she be disappointed? He didn't want that! Edward wanted Meriel Liese to experience what he had experienced. The surprise of the pool itself, its size, the ambience, the mystic, the warmth, and the overwhelming feeling of love and well-being.

Surprisingly Meriel Liese broached the subject, asking if he was looking forward to another seawater bath. Hesitantly he suggested she join him. Meriel Liese visibly wavered, momentarily his heart stopped, sure she was going to say yes! He would have to run down and check the pool if she did while she got herself ready. His anxiety was skyrocketing when Meriel Liese declined, saying, "Perhaps tomorrow night."

Edward internally heaved a sigh of relief, immediately feeling guilt and shame creeping all over him like maggots appearing from nowhere. He thought he needed a bath, a very hot bath.

Diffidently he made his way down to the pool. He was unsure, uncertain, and apprehensive. He wanted it all to himself, like before; still, quiet, undisturbed. Approaching the doors, every muscle in his body tensed. He stopped, gathered himself, relaxed, then with the certainty of a priest leaving the sacristy, cued by the entrance hymn, confidently pushed open the double doors and strode into the pool. The atmosphere was warm and welcoming as two evenings ago, and he had it all to himself.

Drifting dancing shadows filled the spaces between the wall lights. Edward could hear the choir in his head humming. It felt like a profoundly religious experience. Edward was sure she would join him, the woman with the long black hair. He looked around. There wasn't a ripple on the water. She wasn't there yet, but he was sure she would be.

Joyfully, he plunged into the water. It was surprisingly warm. He stretched out, pushed off from the poolside and swam leisurely away, glancing sideways occasionally as he plied the silky water. Edward couldn't see her but sensed her presence. He knew she was there. Her presence was powerful even when out of sight. Robotically swimming lengths, his mind emptied until tiredness overcame him. Turning into his final length, he saw her, waiting for him, it seemed, at the other end of the pool.

She smiled a friendly hello, as he approached and stopped swimming. Breathlessly he matched her smile with his. The woman, with consummate ease, initiated their conversation, asking about Edward's daughter; how she was? What had they been doing? Had she been to the pool yet? Was she enjoying her stay in the hotel? What were their plans? Edward, in turn, told her he thought Meriel Liese looked the better for their stay by the sea and expressed his regret that she hadn't felt disposed to try the pool yet and feared she wouldn't.

"We're leaving on Saturday morning; tomorrow will be her last chance," he confided.

"Tomorrow is the best day to take the pool waters. Don't give up; I'm sure she'll join you," she confidently advised.

Edward felt reassured but didn't know why. There was something sublime about the moment. It reminded him of when he had something serious to confess, leaving the confession box, absolution bestowed, overcome with relief, the burden of guilt removed. They spent a long time chatting, like old friends, before the woman took her leave and swam away.

Later Edward, felt completely at ease as he was getting ready for bed. My swim has done me a world of good, he thought.

Comfortably snug in bed, he drifted off to sleep. Edward didn't see the ribbon of soft moonlight slipping in between the window curtains, moving across his bed as earth and moon performed their orbital dance. He was filled with an intoxicating feeling of well-being.

He was in a small exotic garden. The air was heavy with the scent of flowers. Hearing the splashing sound of water, he turned and saw the water feature. Edward was not alone. Behind the fountain, there was a woman. A dark-haired woman he didn't recognise, but she seemed to know him. Slowly she moved towards him, getting closer and closer. He stepped forward to meet her. A gentle breeze fluffed her hair as she walked. Reaching out his hand to her, she faded away.

Jolting bolt upright in bed, his eyes wide open, the garden, moonlight, and the woman had disappeared. The room clothed in the soft darkness of a July night invited the dream so vivid and intense to linger, but it couldn't. It was gone. He let himself fall back into the crumpled bedsheets, wondering what had spawned his dream. Sleep was slow to return.

Early Friday morning, Edward stood, coffee in hand, on his bedroom balcony watching the sunrise slowly above Island-magee. Feeling energised, he savoured the moment, the rising sun, the fresh sea air, the sounds of the sea birds and the harbour noises. An early morning inbound train would soon be arriving with folk heading to Scotland or the Olderfleet Hotel on summer holiday. As the morning brightened, so did his hopes for Meriel Liese. A shared silence is a sacred thing he was beginning to understand.

They were discussing at breakfast what they might do with their day; take another excursion, go shopping, explore the town, walk along the Coast Road and more, when Megan, her

bright and cheery self, joined them. Their conversation continued as a threesome without resolution until Megan suggested
they join her on a relaxing walking tour as she was very familiar
with the area. Edward was all for it, primarily because Meriel
Liese enjoyed Megan's company.

Shod with footwear suitable for a long walk, they sallied forth
in good heart. They made their way through the harbour , their
lunch destination Ballygally Hotel, from the hotel, quite a distance away. Walking through the port, they stopped to watch the
drama of the mail boat from Stranraer docking. As they walked,
Edward and Meriel Liese didn't notice the distance travelled or
the time passing. Megan, a fountain of local knowledge, pointed
out and commented on everything along the way of interest, including; the town's Jurassic coast, the Viking raids, the building
of the Coast Road, the Black Arch with its Devil's Churn and
the sad story of old Jean Parke, whose mariner husband had
been lost at sea. Old Jean built a makeshift cabin under a seawall
not far from the Black Arch to live in and keep watch for her
husband returning, which he never did. Local people sustained
her with food and other supplies as best they could. She was
warned about a big storm coming but paid no heed. The night
of the storm Old Jean and her makeshift cabin were washed
away, never to be seen again.

At lunch, Megan told them all about the ghost of the Ballygally Castle Hotel and that they might even get a chance to climb
up the turret to the haunted room. Meriel Liese wasn't too keen
on meeting a ghost. She told them about the Spanish chestnut
tree in the church grounds not too far up the road from where
they were. Megan then launched into an explanation of how the
Spanish chestnut tree grew there and the plight of the Spanish
Armada. It was the recovery of a Spanish sailor's body, buried
with a chestnut in his pocket, in the church grounds she told

them that produced the Spanish chestnut tree. She captivated her companions.

After lunch, they had their coffee in the lounge, where they could enjoy the panoramic views afforded by the picture windows around three sides of the room. Edward was glad to sit down for a while. His nearly new shoes were nibbling at his heels, particularly the right one. The heavy scent of purposefully placed tubs of roses in full bloom filled the cool lounge. Meriel Liese closed her eyes, inhaling the heady aroma, as the mail boat nosed its way out of the mouth of Larne Harbour, steering for Stranraer.

Megan sat by the open window watching the boat, the sea breeze ruffling her hair, raising her head as if to taste the tang of the sea, listening to its murmurings, observing the changing patchwork hues of greens and blues, floating on the surface. She was absorbed. So intent, it was as if she was searching for something. Meriel Liese pointed to the departing mail boat. Megan focusing on the ship explained how the Captain depending on winds, currents and tides, steered different arcing courses to use the currents to good purpose.

Edward listening as she spoke, reflecting on their walk along the Coast Road and her knowledge of the sea, was tempted to ask if she was a mariner. He let the temptation pass. Meriel Liese, he noticed, had colour in her cheeks. She was glowing. Full it seemed of expectation. There was even a hint of excitement. He remembered when being her age with a decision to make, to stay in the past or embrace the future; take the chance was his choice. It was like when a boy stood knees knocking on tiptoe to dive for the first time into the swimming hole in the river at home while other veteran divers urged him on. Looking again at Meriel Liese, he felt she was at a point of transition; she didn't show it, Edward sensed it.

The day had eased into mid-afternoon as they started back to their hotel. Edward was at times like the unwanted person in a threesome as Megan, and his daughter talked all the way back to their hotel. At Waterloo Bay and the limestone kilns they paused and rested while taking the view. They were tired, but it had been an enjoyable day. *A day well spent all-round,* Edward thought. Edward invited Megan to join them for dinner, but unfortunately, she couldn't, some things needed her attention, "Maybe later perhaps," she said.

Edward didn't press her further, grateful for the day in her company.

In the dining room, early as usual for the first sitting, with the choice of tables, they took their usual one from which they could scan the room in relative privacy. There was a freshness in the air that Edward couldn't quite put his finger on. He and Meriel Liese casually dressed in keeping with the hotel's dress code, as were some of the guests he recognised, and others he didn't were more formally attired.

Then he realised that the freshness was associated with the new arrivals, unsure about the dining room protocols, exhibiting their uncertainty. It was all part of the guest ebb and flow in hotels, the filling and emptying and refilling during the height of the season. Another thing that added anticipation was the Friday night's free entertainment. They chatted about their week and their long walk as they ate, while keeping an eye on what was happening around them. Sometimes conversation lulled. They were comfortable with each other, they didn't have to keep talking, and they could enjoy the richness of their shared silence.

During one of those lulls, Edward asked Meriel Liese if she would like to come down later for the entertainment. She thought about it for a little while. He could see the gears churning in her mind. Setting her cutlery neatly beside her plate, she turned to him and said, "I feel too tired for that, but a visit to the seawater baths might be the more relaxing option."

"An excellent suggestion. A seawater bath might be the best for both of us." Edward replied enthusiastically.

Edward hadn't mentioned the seawater bath at breakfast, didn't mention it all on their walk and was loathe raising it at dinner, but he was surprised and delighted Meriel Liese had now. Was she in the process of casting off her overburdening grief? He didn't know, but something was happening; Meriel Liese was going because she wanted to. What if the pool is full of other people? Anxiety started bubbling inside him again, like water in a pot about to boil over. Over dessert and coffee, he managed to hide the eruption of feelings inside him.

In his room, waiting for Meriel Liese to join him, Edward stood on the balcony looking across the Lough. There was no noise, only a strange silence and unease that he couldn't shake off settled on his shoulders. Edward pressed fingers to his pulsating temple, counting the pulses, breathing deeply and slowly, desperately trying to suppress his escalating anxiety.

The connecting door opened, Edward turning faced his daughter and managed to smile. She looked radiant. Joining her father on the balcony, Meriel Liese was unaware of his inner turmoil, and all he hoped for was that she would experience what he had experienced on his first visit to the seawater pool.

In matching dressing gowns, courtesy of the hotel, they made their way along the backstairs corridor leading down to the basement. It was as if the hotel was asleep, silent. As they walked, Edward's left-hand unconsciously patted his thigh. Walking on his right Meriel Liese didn't notice. The pat – pat – pat tempo, increased as they descended the stairs.

Then they were in the corridor leading to the pool. The double doors were closed, and it was deadly quiet. A hush settled on

Edward. An anxious hush. He was praying that there would be no one in the pool and that they would have it all to themselves. He paused before the doors, afraid to breathe, and bracing himself, swung them open, cowardly inviting his daughter to enter first. Meriel Liese confidently walked through, expecting seawater baths. Edward hanging back, greatly relieved, saw that it was just as it was on his first visit.

Meriel Liese was astonished. She was expecting a bath, not a swimming pool. Standing in awe, she watched the mysterious shadows dancing between the lights on the tiled walls and ceiling. Edward stood beside her as she took it all in. She couldn't believe it. In the middle of the pool, the water rippled gently. The kind of rippling that forms concentric circles when a small pebble is dropped into water. They didn't notice it, but something was stirring the water.

Meriel Liese was hesitant to enter the pool. She thought it would be cold. Edward, anxiety dispelled, eagerly jumped in. The water was not cold; it was like seawater on a hot summer's day at the beach. Warily Meriel Liese joined him. Pleasantly surprised, she fully immersed and swam away. Her thankful father, watching his daughter swimming, followed in her wake.

Swimming, Edward sensed another presence in the pool. Glancing from side to side, he saw nothing. Underwater glancing side to side, he saw nothing. The feeling grew stronger. Meriel Liese glided effortlessly through the water, changing strokes at will. Edward resting at the side of the pool watched. He was sure they were the only ones there, yet the feeling of another presence persisted. Edward's contemplative mood invited Dvorak's song, that his mother often played, came to mind; 'Songs My Mother Taught Me.' Humming the music, he recalled the lyrics;

'Songs my mother taught me,
In the deep days long vanished,
Seldom from her eyelids
Were teardrops banished.

Now I teach my children,
Each melodious measure,
Oft the tears are flowing,'
Oft they flow from my memory's treasure.'

Opening his eyes, he watched Meriel Liese swimming down the pool away from him. He thought for a moment; *there's someone in the water with her, there can't be! Can there? I'm imagining it; it's a shadow, is it?* Rubbing his eyes to refocus, his daughter turned and swam towards him. He saw nothing in the water beside her. On her return length down the pool, his eyes on her, he saw it again, a shadow, a fish-shaped shadow. A big fish! He leapt to his feet, ready to jump in to his daughter's aid. Reason intervened. *There couldn't be a fish in the pool, could there?* Edward was standing in the water when Meriel reached him and stood up beside him, beaming.

"If I'd known it was this good, I'd have been down here every day; it's great."

Her father, as father's do, smiling gave her his 'I told so' look.

"I'd love to stay longer, but ...

"Let's do another couple lengths together before we go," Edward suggested.

They swam another ten lengths, during which he scanned the floor of the pool for any sign of anything that shouldn't have been there and might have floated upwards. There was nothing. He looked for a fish but didn't see any, but the feeling that they were not alone wouldn't leave him.

When they got out of the pool, the water stilled. It felt as if Edward and Meriel Liese were in a temple of listening, lost in a treasury of deep sacred silence. Closing the pool doors behind them, Edward had a last fleeting look around. There was no one there. In their rooms, before they said goodnight, Meriel Liese hugged her father, saying, "Thank you, father, that was spectacular; I should have gone with you earlier, you showed me the way, but I just wasn't ready."

Edward usually so self-controlled let his feelings show. "I thought I was losing you," he managed through clenched teeth before tears drenched his face.

"Never, Father. Never."

They talked long into the night before tiredness summoned them to sleep. Edward didn't go to bed; he stepped out onto his balcony. Under a cloudless star-filled sky, he raised his eyes heavenward in silent thanksgiving.

Megan joined them for breakfast. As soon as she sat down, Meriel Liese, exuberantly in a flood of words, told her all about her visit to the seawater pool, finishing with, "It was amazing, absolutely amazing. I wish I had gone with father earlier, and now we're leaving this morning."

"But sure, now you know it's there, you can come back and enjoy it anytime. You got the best day for it."

The two girls continued talking with Meriel Liese doing most of it; Megan listened intently and spoke little. A spectator at the breakfast table, Edward thought, *I'm witnessing my daughter unlocking her inner grief. Soon I hope the work of grieving in her will be complete. Last night was transformative for both of us.* He felt his anxieties about Meriel Liese's health and wellbeing melting away.

The moment of parting and going their separate ways arrived too soon. Edward and Meriel Liese would start their journey home on the eleven o'clock train. Megan, smiling, said, "I've some more exploring to do down the coast. I'll call in at Dunluce Castle; I always like being close to the sea."

On the train home, Meriel Liese read. Edward, eyes closed, pondered on their short vacation and all that had happened. It seemed like a dream, but it wasn't. Looking at his daughter, he could see a difference, a transformation. To him, she was like a rose in spring about to burst into blossom. With colour in her cheeks, a sparkle in her eyes, Meriel Liese had a cheeriness about her she didn't have before. There would be no need for a posse of physicians to cure her ailment. She'd managed that herself, somehow.

There's more,

Her great grandfather's notes ended there. Mary wondered what the 'more' could be. Reading through the notes several times, she discovered an interesting fact. All of the females' forenames had the initial M. *That's kind of quirky,* she thought. *Is there a family connection here? Could Muriel in the notes be my great-great-grandmother? Did my great-great-grandfather work in the Olderfleet Hotel?'*

Something else grabbed her attention. The Friday that Meriel Liese entered the seawater pool in the Olderfleet Hotel was the 23rd of July, the exact date LiBan was pulled from the Inver River and baptised by Saint Comgall when he bestowed on her the name Muirgen – sea-born.

Sat with her laptop open, Mary thought, *is it just a coincidence? Is there more to all of this? It's time I found out. But where to start? Ancestry? Why not? I'll build the family tree first and see where that leads us.*

The cursor blinking on her laptop screen waited for her to start tapping.

The Mill Street Matchmaker

Larne in the eighteenth-century consisted of two discrete parts; the 'Old Town' and the 'New Town.' A distinction, persisting as long as living memory allows. In an area of Gardenmore, on the west side, the 'Old Town', described as being 'ill-built, poorly `edificed, irregularly aligned with narrow, crooked thorough-fares, as to present a disagreeable appearance', was a neighbour-hood with distinctive attributes.

Mill Street, its main thoroughfare, was the backbone of a web of streets and lanes named in honour of the various mills oper-ating beside the Larne River that throbbed and bustled, provid-ing employment. Eventually, the mills gave way to a clothing factory, employing women, sewing, stitching, pressing and pack-aging garments. The glazed roof flooded their workspace with daylight. In winter, it was cold, in summer like an oven. It was a noisy environment; some women wore cotton plugs in their ears, their work output closely monitored. The sweatshop of its day, it enabled women to put food on their tables.

The factory horn punctuated their lives, summoning them to early morning work, blaring again, at midday twice, signalling the beginning and end of the short lunchtime break, and again, at six pm to release them home, yearning for peace and quiet, their day's work done, for another day. The clickity-clacking of noisy sewing machines reverberated around the neighbourhood all day, and the hissing of the steam-driven pressing machines, made the factory sound like a giant beast, alive – breathing. Coal-fed boilers fired up every morning, spewing black smoke from the hexagonal, red-bricked chimney, blanketing the neighbourhood until swept away by prevailing winds.

Coopers noisily plied their trade, making tubs, piggins, noggins, barrels churns, coops for housing poultry, washtubs and all-purpose use containers, in the aptly named Coopers Lane. Retired whiskey barrels, filled with water for purification, produced a liquor, strong enough to sustain the coopers, happily at their work, for days on end. It also gave the lane its distinct aroma. Mission Lane, dubbed Methodist Lane, after John Wesley preached there, was an acquired label too. So it was for all the lanes, mill races and knowes, that constituted the Old Town.

But it was a vibrant, lively, cheerful, noisy place, blessed with a distinctive character and an abundance of colourful inhabitants rubbing shoulders, living cheek by jowl, day by day. Long before the 'Big Apple', the 'Old Town' never slept.

Mill Street, in truth, the Old Town's artery, bounded by lanes, was where the business and professional people lived. Substantial dwellings, both sides of the road, hedged it. Renowned poets Drummond, McCoy and McHenry resided there, as did others, meriting mention in other professions. By contrast, the insubstantial dwellings in the lanes bounding Mill Street housed the working classes.

It was a diverse, variegated, harmonious, socially stratified community. This microcosmic, eclectic, societal mix fostered a dynamic, caring community ultimately scattered in the 1960s when the neighbourhood, under the banner of regeneration, was demolished

Yet before that end came, and back as the area developed, Mill Street, where it joined Bridge Street and Dunluce Street, was anchored by Whiteside's drapery and Longmore's hardware stores, respectively. The Johnston family owned Longmore's store, and their son James was the principal tenor at the Royal Opera House in London for years. In retirement, he occasionally served in the store, frequently entertaining patrons with renditions of operatic arias. There were butchers, bakers, greengrocers, sweetie shops, pet shops, pork and bacon stores supplied by McCormick slaughtering pigs in his back yard, public houses and grocers. Victuallers, including those licensed to sell spirits, were plentiful.

Two Garvey sisters owned The Beehive, a very select public house frequented by discerning patrons with a premium on privacy to meet and imbibe, watched over by the resident parrot and cockatoo. Above them, furniture restorers liberally applied their polishes, perfuming the air. Other licensed public houses, including Mossey's and the Crown Bar, competed with several unlicensed premises with colourful nicknames purveying liquors of the home-distilled variety. Licensed spirit and wine merchants plied their trades in Ferris and Mission Lanes too.

It was a busy, bustling, effervescent place that never slept. Mrs Wilson's broth was available all day, as were Mrs Henderson's potted herrings, and for those homeward bound from the public houses, roasted pig's feet was the fast-food takeaway of choice. Coal sold by the stone, buttermilk by the pint, as was porter and paint. Newlyweds furnished their homes with second-hand furniture from Johnny Johnston's store. When the shops closed on a Saturday at 11 pm, the street was chock-a-block with people waiting for the sixpenny roll-up, when the butchers, bakers and others with victuals, that won't last the weekend, sold them off at bargain prices. This drama happened

every Saturday night in Mill Street, thronging with eager partici-
pants, curtain up, 11 pm on the dot. There was a carnival atmosphere, the air laden with intoxicating aromas of roasted pig's
feet, simmering broth, steaming tripe and onions and bowels of
cockles and mussels.

The Old Town, a melting pot of humanity, residing on streets
and lanes in substantial houses and single-storey, rubble-built,
whitewashed rows of small dwellings, exuding harmony amidst
the travails of life and a community spirit, sacrificed on the altar
of redevelopment. Now beyond resurrection.

John Clifford's poem 'Mill Street' igniting imagination, places
its characters centre stage:

'As I went up the Mill Street
and feeling very grand,
stepping right and proudly
with a shilling in my hand.
I knew that nearly everything
I wanted would be there,
and when I'd finished buying
I'd have money still to spare.'

Sadly it is only in memory and imagination that it is possible to
walk and experience something no longer tangible.

The Old Town, full of many colourful, larger than life characters, in plain sight, had others whose unassuming natures gave
no hint of involvement in affairs of the heart.

Barry McGrogan was one such person. He never married,
lived alone, simply, in a non-descript dwelling in 'The Knowe' –
a variation of knoll or hillock dating back to the 16th century –
and made his living by way of his small flatbed truck, he affectionately called 'his wee three tonner'. If asked what he did for a
living, he would answer quietly, in an offhand, disarming, kind

of way, "Oh, just a bit of this and that, whatever comes along, you know?" Suggesting total reliance on God's benevolence.

Clean and tidy at home and in his daily business, he was medium in height and build, always well-groomed, an open square face housing dancing eyes; didn't smoke or drink and walked straight-backed and square-shouldered. He wore dungarees and laced-up boots for his daily work unless the job in hand demanded other attire. Barry, always cheerful, with a word for everyone he met, walked on the balls of his dancing feet, light and graceful as a ballet dancer.

If something needed shifting, Barry was the man for the job. No job was too small. He toured the town every day, routinely, looking for work. He travelled around the countryside on the same mission, buying anything he thought would turn a profit in the reselling, scrap metal, bits of machinery, furniture and pictures. He would say that the unwanted, especially the unloved, was his interest – always more profit in anything unloved. He had a small yard off Albert Street where he kept his stock. That's how Barry earned his daily bread – doing a bit of this and a bit of that. He was well enough off, owned his own wee house, the place on Albert Street, and the wee three tonner – there weren't many of them on the road in those days.

In his working-class way, Barry was an astute businessman; his osprey eyes scanned the lives of the people he met every day, looking for a bit of business. He could read people. Barry was very friendly, easy to talk to, had tea in many houses, sharing confidences while eliciting information. He wasn't a wicked person; it wasn't in his nature, far from it. Barry used the information gleaned to help people. He was, in many ways, a good Samaritan who would do anybody a good turn if he could.

His home, the middle one in the row of three on The Knowe, blessed with an envious aspect, overlooking the Inver River that flowed through the seasons below him to the sea. Larne Lough bounded by Islandmagee on one shore and the tree-covered slopes of the Inver Bares on the other, flowed and ebbed with the pull of the moon. Raising his eyes, looking up over the Bleach and Dye works, the green pastures of the Inver Plateau collided with the changing sky. *It is an ever-changing panorama that must have coloured the lives of the Friars of Invermore as it colours mine,* Barry often thought standing, taking it all in.

Families lived on either side of him. On his right a family of seven, the parents, four boys and a girl. The girl Rosie, piggy in the middle of four boys, was nineteen, worked in the mill near the bottom of Mill Street, of a quiet disposition, spent most of her time helping her ailing mother and looking after her father and brothers. The family on his left had three boisterous young children; Barry found entertaining on manys a summer evening.

Sometimes of an evening, Saturday afternoon, Sunday morning, Barry would, a mug of tea in hand, sit outside on the wall overlooking the river, slowly negotiating its way to the sea, occasionally lifting his head looking around, thinking his thoughts. Sometimes, Rosie from next door joined him, tea in hand – for a breath of air – she would say. She was a lovely girl, dressed plainly, with no airs or graces about her. Barry liked her company. They would chat, about nothing in particular, though all the while, Barry couldn't help but feel that Rosie was searching for something. It took him some time to figure out that Rosie, raised in a male environment, and used to having men about the place, had girlfriends but no boyfriends. She, content in herself, didn't need them, it seemed.

Barry liked to fish the Inver River for brown and sea trout. It was a pastime he shared with his young friend, Bobby. One Saturday afternoon, sitting outside sipping his tea, Barry waited for Bobby to go fishing when Rosie, cup in hand, joined him.

Shortly after that, Bobby arrived, fishing tackle shouldered and ready. Barry made the introductions, Rosie, hospitable to a fault, insisted she fetch Bobby some tea. The threesome sat, Barry in the middle, drinking their tea and chatting until it was time for Barry and Bobby to head upriver fishing. In the weeks that followed, their chance meeting became a frequent occurrence such that chance could be ignored.

As Rosie and Bobby got to know each other, she discovered that he lived just a few hundred yards away, around the corner in Black's Lane. There was nothing unusual in that, children went to different faith schools, so there weren't that many opportunities to meet socially. Rosie, with family commitments, didn't go out much anyway. Their chance meeting with Barry that Saturday, the cup of tea and chat, was the prelude to marriage, following which locals in the know anointed Barry with the title, The Mill Street Matchmaker.

Barry wasn't a matchmaker, not even a facilitator, but he did encourage Rosie and Bobby's relationship. His young friend was a fine upstanding lad, and Rosie, cut from the same cloth, had a caring heart. Barry knew they had found their soul mates.

Barry's anointment as the Mill Street Matchmaker, intended as a joke set firm. Around the lanes, children followed him rhyming – Barry, Barry, who'll you marry – big Maggie and wee Harry – tiny Mina and lanky Wharry – he felt like the Pied Piper, but took it all for the fun that was in it, enjoying his newfound fame. Going about earning his daily bread, in and out of people's houses, sipping tea and chatting, he paid more attention to the home environment, making a point of engaging the sons and daughters in conversation at every opportunity. Intuitively Barry was creating a database; character traits, integrity, sincerity, tolerance, determination, loyalty, devotion, all feeding into the matching matrix budding in his head. *It's only a bit of a game,* he thought.

Serendipity matched Rosie and Bobby; Barry, a friend to both, was a passive participant. In the matches that followed, Barry was the active ingredient, the yeast in the dough.

Word of Barry's matchmaking success with Rosie and Bobby crept over the countryside like a morning mist. People sought his services. At first reluctant, Barry yielded to persuasion, some desperate, and tried his hand at matchmaking. His first two matches were easy. The couples in question knew each other; their families knew each other too; the boys and girls in their late twenties, having never mastered the art of courting, didn't know how to make the first move. All Barry had to do was give a bit of a nudge, and the matches were made.

Shortly after taking up the delicate art of matchmaking, two successes under his belt, a lady in her late thirties asked Barry to find her a match. She was single, lived alone hadn't been married before. Taking her at face value, a mistake he never made again, he set about finding her a match and found one. Sadly they were only a few years married when the husband passed away. Barry found her another partner. He soon passed away too. Barry discovered that she was a good for nothing charlatan, couldn't cook nor keep a house, and when she came looking for a third match, Barry showed her the door. His parting words were, "Missus, never pour water on a drowned mouse."

That was Barry's baptism into the real world of matchmaking, his only failure and his first lesson – do your homework – know your client – be professional. Matchmaking he learned demanded, in addition to knowledge of character traits, remarkable tact, sensitivity, a delicate touch and a moral code. Barry slowly, carefully, morphed into his burgeoning but minor persona. Minor it may have been, but not the sort of undertaking to be performed in dungarees.

His matchmaker garb was a white open-necked shirt, a black V-necked pullover, black corduroy trousers, brown laced boots, a tweed jacket, and on his head a blackcap set at a rakish angle. Although he never smoked, he chose to have a pipe in his hand; it made him look sage, he thought and was helpful as a tool to emphasize a point when needed. On occasions, whenever he felt like it, he wore eyeglasses for characterisation. A blackthorn walking stick in hand added weight to authenticity. Barry's matchmaker outfit was transforming; he became a different person. His facial features wizened, blue eyes twinkled, furrowed brows conveyed wisdom; he became elfish like, with a mischievous, beguiling smile.

Barry's occupation and personality equipped him for his matchmaker's role. He had a foot in the Old Town, the New Town and out and around in the townlands, a man of many feet, urban and rural, it could be said. Blessed, he was too, with the gift of the gab. Visiting dwellings, urban or rural, made no difference; he could easily carry gossip, dispensing it, flavoured to suit the recipient's ear, but never with malicious intent. Just for the fun that was in it. Barry never spoke ill of anyone, avoiding arguments, by agreeing with what folk said, with the odd caveat, "Ah, sure, your right there, never a truer word spoken, couldn't agree more."

He had a bucketful of get out of difficulty sayings that issued effortlessly from his tongue. Barry could charm the birds out of their nests.

Maturing in the art of matchmaking, he realised he was really in the business of conveying secret and intimate heart messages from one party to another. Discretion was the name of the game, and he was, in essence, Cupid's facilitator. Barry soon realised that many men were particularly undernourished and desperately unrehearsed in the language of love. They didn't have the vocabulary and the energy essential for the expressions of an open heart. Growing into his profession, he acquired knowledge of character hitherto beyond his aspiration, filling out the matchmaking matrix in his head. Occasionally delicacy was required, sometimes a gentle thrust sufficed, now and again a shove was the needed catalyst.

Some, in rural areas, married for land, others married for love. Many a young woman, who had married an older man for his land, lived to regret it, as their older spouse aged long before their eyes, harbouring thoughts that they never thought they would own. Barry, wary of such matches, trod carefully.

Common to both urban and rural matters of the heart is the driving desire for parents in making a match for the betterment and wellbeing of their offspring. Barry understood that. He would have no truck with anyone making a match for land, "No good could come of it," he would say in dismissal.

Of course, there was always the matter of the settlement. It never ceased to amaze him how a mother of little means could so miserly haggle over the payment until he realised she simply wanted something more for her child than she ever had. A better start in life.

Often a family would avail of Barry's services. Other times he would bump into someone accidentally, of course, and engage in conversation. He was a kind of Jumping Jenny, with a slow-burning fuse, which when ignited would set about charming the one and then the other, awakening nascent romantic longings.

When Barry met big Dan O'Conner one day, by chance, he greeted him like a long lost son. "Dan, how are you doing, old son?"

"Not so bad Barry, how's yourself?"

"All right, I suppose, if it wasn't for me old back and the pain that's in it. How's your mother doing? The last time we spoke, she was having a bit of back trouble too. I hope the pain has passed, poor woman?"

"Not a bother on her, Barry, thanks be to God, she never stops cleaning and tidying, sure you know what's she's like, never sits still."

"I'm mighty glad to hear that Dan, she's a goer right enough, a great woman and well thought of too. She worked in the vicarage in Ballyloran before she married your father. Didn't the Reverent and his missus give them their wedding breakfast up there? That's how well your mother was regarded. What's the news with you, Dan?"

"I didn't know that Barry, that's news to me."

Barry closing in on his quarry would not be side-tracked. "And what about you, Dan, what's your news,"

Barry had done his homework on Dan, the eldest of his siblings, with a couple younger than himself married and left home. He came from good stock, had a good job, and was easy going, mild-mannered, and thrifty, but lacking in the lexicon of romance.

"What news would I have now, Barry? Sure it's yourself that's always talking to people, and you'd have more news than what's in the paper!"

"Ah, now Dan sure you never spoke a truer word. Wasn't I speaking to a friend of mine about yourself just the other day?"

"Who would that be, Barry?"

"A friend, Dan a friend of mine that speaks highly of you. You have more friends than you think, Dan, friends that any man would be glad of."

"And who would this friend be then Barry?"

Dan had taken Barry's bait, hook, line, and sinker.

"Dan, isn't she the nicest young woman you'd ever set eyes

on? Nothing's too good for that girl, I'm telling you, one in a million, but very shy. Tell him yourself say's I, sure where would you get the likes of Dan O Conner? Molly McKeown's a lovely girl, Dan. She'll be at the dance in the church hall on Saturday night."

Dan, retreating into himself, feigned indifference.

Barry, Dan's interest piqued, took his leave with a knowing glance, letting his news ferment. That's how big Dan O'Conner got to learn about Molly McKeown's interest.

With the seed planted in big Dan's mind, Barry accidentally, of course, bumped into Molly and engaged her in conversation, in the process letting her know that big Dan had mentioned her and that he would be at the dance in the church hall. A matching seed planted, a few more accidental encounters, if needed, to move things along, during which Barry would caress and convey intimate matters of the heart, with a furrowed brow, a hint of a smile, and a touch of the hand. It was for the matchmaker, work in progress, cultivating a relationship that would develop and mature into lasting wedlock when the settlement was made. In trifling matters, he would counsel in his imitable way, "Inches disnae break squares in a load o'whins, you know."

Barry never sought payment for his services. He was that kind of person. It is beyond imagination to comprehend how happy Barry was helping people, reliant on God's providence and without a care in the world. Careful about his calling, he would not pursue a match if he perceived a character flaw in either potential participant. He would never match a mean man with a decent woman. Barry had his code of ethics. That was another column in his matchmaking matrix.

One day, he went up to a farmhouse in Ballyboley, at the behest of the farmer, searching for a match for his only child, a daughter, who had no interest in men nor to all intents and purposes marriage. Stooping under the lintel, eyes on the floor, Barry entered the house. He was in a big front room, fire burning brightly in the grate; walls lined with dressers, and in the middle of the room, standing aproned, at a scrubbed pine table baking, was the most beautiful young woman he had ever laid his eyes on. She looked up, smiling warmly at him, as Barry stood in speechless wonderment. Realising he was staring, he smiled, hiding his awe. He was sure she could hear his heart pounding, notice his breast heaving, see his face colouring. Barry had never experienced this exciting, heady, confusing feeling before. Enraptured, he didn't realise that Cupid's dart had pierced his heart.

Introductions made, her father busied himself outside while her mother, seating them in front of the fire, served tea and homemade soda cake before finding something to do in the back room. Barry, tingling inside, reluctant to reach for the mug of tea, lest a shaky hand reveal his inner turmoil, clasped them tightly, prayerfully. Jennifer opposite Barry, looking directly at him, knowing he was there because her parents, with her consent, had arranged the meeting, opened their conversation, with a dreamy sort of smile, asking, "What can I do for you, then, Sir?"

Barry, momentarily lost, swimming in her deep luminous brown eyes, managed, "I'm not sure yet, to be honest."

Their exploratory conversation continued for an hour before her father reappeared, bringing proceedings to a close. Another meeting arranged two weeks later; Barry took his leave with much to ponder.

The meeting had not gone as Barry expected. He assumed he would lead the conversation, trying to obtain a character profile from Jennifer for a suitable match. But Jennifer took the lead.

Barry had never been interviewed for a job or anything else in his life, but when they had finished, he had been thoroughly quizzed, subtly given the third degree and gently put through the wringer.

Barry arrived on time at the farmhouse for their second meeting.

"Jennifer's out walking the dogs; she'll be back any minute," her mother explained, greeting him at the door. "Come in and make yourself at home. I'll have tea for you in a minute; sure, the kettle's always on the boil."

Barry was hardly settled in his seat by the fire when Jennifer burst into the room full of apologies for her tardiness. Barry didn't hear her. He was looking at her, standing looking down at him, wellington boots on her feet, the bottom of her sky blue jeans tucked in, slate grey jacket half unbuttoned and her wind-blown auburn hair in disarray. She looked stunning. Jennifer broke the spell, "Give me a minute, please, and I'll be right with you," she said, rushing off.

A few minutes later, she returned, her hair tidied up, minus the wellington boots and jacket.

Barry waved Jennifer's more fulsome apology away and got down to business. Determined at this meeting to be in the driving seat, Barry started gently obtaining from Jennifer what she would be looking for in an ideal match. Looking him in the eyes, she responded without hesitation, "Integrity, someone I can trust, someone I can rely on."

As the conversation continued, Barry noted the expressions Jennifer used in his mind: kind and caring, cheerful, good conservationist, loving, loyal, respectful and tolerant, sense of fun, and many more. Jennifer, in her mind, knew what she wanted and wouldn't settle for less. Barry discerned that and more; Jennifer wanted fidelity.

Barry sat on the wall, tea in hand at home in the Knowe, looking down into the river flowing far below. The swirls, eddies and turbulence caused by rocks disturbing the fluency of the flowing water summed up for Barry exactly how he was feeling, wrapped in a whirl, thinking, dreaming of Jennifer!

"Don't be daft, Barry; you're off your rocker, get a grip; she's only a child, half your age, for goodness sake." He scolded himself and lashed the dregs in his mug over the wall towards the river.

They met twice in Jennifer's home the following month, her parents in close attendance. Pursuing a suitable match for Jennifer had become a complex, painful undertaking for Barry. He couldn't bring himself to look her directly in the eyes for fear of the blushing under his shirt collar, creeping out, revealing all. He could feel her watching him, not glancing, searching. She the light, he the moth circling it, drawn to it irresistibly. His integrity at risk Barry questioned his motives – maybe he wasn't trying hard enough to find Jennifer a match.

Barry sat before the fire in the big room opposite Jennifer, for what he thought would be their final meeting, unaware that their roles had reversed again. He began the conversation, waffling on about things peripheral to matters at hand. Losing patience, Jennifer candidly interrupted asking, "Barry, have you any news for me?"

Friends, now they could speak frankly.

"Do you want the bad news or good news, Jennifer?"

"Whatever news you've got will do."

"The good news is that any man, in the country, with an acorn of a brain would want you, Jennifer. There's no doubt about that. Unfortunately, the bad news is, I can't find one worthy of you," Barry honestly told her.

"Sure, your bad news – you can't find one – is good news for me, and as for your good news, I wouldn't take the want of any man in the country, except one of my choosing."

At that, Barry perked up, clutching for straws, "And what would he be like, I wonder, tell me?" Barry asked, desperate for guidance.

"There's a saying around here, Barry, I'm sure you've heard it – look for a thing till ye find it, an' then ye'll not lose your labour."

Jennifer sat for a moment, looking at the bewilderment in his eyes. "Sure, don't you yet know it? Don't you know Barry McGrogan – it's you I want!"

Her love declared, the offer of marriage was absolute. At ease, in control of the situation, Jennifer sat back in her chair, allowing Barry time to absorb the solemnity and magnificence of the moment. She had stripped him of his theatrical persona, exposing his hidden authentic self.

Stunned, he stared through vacant eyes at her in utter disbelief, muttering, "Go on, Jennifer, you can't be serious; pull the other leg."

When his shattered senses reset, he realised she was sure, very sure. It wasn't every day a woman as independent as Jennifer proposed marriage to someone.

"Barry, it's no leg-pull. What do you think I've been doing since we first met, eh? I'll tell you. I've been running my eye over you. Getting to know and fall in love with you. Don't be disappointing me now, Barry, say yes."

Barry wanted with all his heart to say yes, but being the decent man he was, Barry planted every obstacle he could think of in their way: age difference – he was twenty years older than her.

"You have a few nicks on your horn all right, but the older the fiddle sure, the sweeter the tune! Isn't that something you've often said to others, Barry?" she laughed.

"Your parents, what will they think?"

"They'll be delighted," came back her assurance, "they know you're not a land grabber."

"People will talk!"

"Sure, if they're talking about us, won't they be leaving other people alone, and I might as well be hung for an auld sheep as a lamb," Jennifer countered.

Eventually, his defences breached, eyes glittering brightly, face flushed, Barry surrendered his heart to Jennifer's love, a dreamy smile shunting away his wizened look. In the quiet solemnity of the room, before the fire, looking deep into her caramel-coloured eyes, kneeling, he confessed, "Jennifer, the first time I saw your face, my heart skipped a beat; I knew I was falling in love with you, but I was conflicted. My feeble resistance was pathetic. I love you. I want to be with you always."

"I know Barry; you were so transparent and sincere it showed – my parents read it in your face."

Jennifer knelt, leant forward and kissed Barry; they knelt holding hands, in the wonder of the moment. Barry was floating on a sea of unbelievable joy and happiness when Jennifer's father entering affirmed he wasn't dreaming.

Outside, parting at the gate, Barry suggested a cooling-off period before telling her parents in case – he didn't get any further – Jennifer said, "They already know Barry! They're not daft, you know, would twenty-four hours be long enough?"

They kissed again. Barry bounced, happy as a sandboy, all the way back to the Knowe.

Jennifer's parents were delighted with the match Jennifer had made. Tongues wagged, of course, but that didn't bother Jennifer and Barry. A few months later, they married, lived below the radar and raised a family. They belonged together. It was the only encounter in Barry's matchmaking career that he was mis-matched, outmanoeuvred and hoisted high on his own petard.

Barry continued his matchmaking with Jennifer's help from the farm in Ballyboley. He was reluctant to leave his home in the Knowe overlooking the Inver River. He never wanted or made a halfpenny from matchmaking, but he surely was rewarded in a way he could never have anticipated. You could say God was good to him.

Barry and his like are an extinct species now, dating agencies, their lacklustre, inferior substitutes. Suppose you're ever up at the head of the town looking over Riverdale – the name given, to the emptiness replacing Mill Street and its interconnected web of lanes, races and knowes, you'll see a row of lock-up garages, where Mossey's pub used to be. You might still get a faint smell of stale porter. To the left beside them, the stump of the clothing factory's red-bricked, hexagonal chimney proudly bears witness to the resilient, variegated, caring community that once was its heart and soul.

As Clifford's poem concludes:
'You may talk about your Main Street
Your Cross Street or Dunluce,
There's not a thing in one of them
That Mill Street can't produce.
They're very grand up Inver
And Roddens and Clonlee,
But the kindly folk of Mill Street
Are good enough for me.'

Spare a thought, too, for the Mill Street Matchmaker who gifted rich colour to the palette of the Old Town.

A Tin Hut Home

Billy Kelly flew Concorde from New York to London for a series of business meetings. It was a trip he had made many times. Boarding, he quickly found his window seat. A rather large rotund man occupying the aisle seat stood to let Billy into his and then unceremoniously plopped back down and buckled up. Settled, Billy fastened his seat belt, leant back in his seat and unwittingly rested his right arm on his neighbour's surplus corpulence, squeezed upwards and outwards by compressive forces. His neighbour didn't acknowledge the trespassing arm, which Billy sheepishly removed.

"Hi, I'm Bob," his fellow traveller said, offering Billy a plump hand.

"I'm Billy," Billy responded, grasping the huge paw.

Introductions made, conversation easily flowed. Bob spoke with a soft, lazy southern drawl that was easy on the ear. He liked to talk and was easy listening to on a wide range of topics. It didn't seem to matter what tangential observation Billy made; Bob would eloquently continue the discourse analysing the pros and cons before advancing an opinion. Conversation over breakfast continued unabated, with Bob doing most of the talking. In no time at all, it seemed they were landing in London.

Disembarking Concorde Bob and Billy exchanged goodbyes and went their separate ways.

This trip was different because, on this occasion, Billy had included free time in his itinerary to do something he had wanted to do for a long time. Three days of intensive business meetings concluded he said goodbye to London and flew Air Lingus to Belfast, hired a car and drove north to Larne.

Billy, a war baby born in 1940, emigrated to the United States of America when he was twenty-seven, and this was his first visit back home.

Driving north, infrastructural changes were everywhere. Motorways and dual carriageways replacing narrow hedge-lined roads made driving less frustrating and saved a great deal of time. Time was money to Billy. *This place has prospered and moved on,* he thought.

Approaching Larne, he followed the dual carriageway signage, negotiated his way through a series of roundabouts before leaving the Harbour Highway to connect with the Glenarm Road. At the traffic lights, new to him, paused on red, at the junction of Curran Road and Main Street, he noted the war memorial was missing, as was the Latharna Hotel. But he knew the hotel wasn't in business anymore because he had tried to make a reservation. Billy was staring at its replacement, an apartment block, when a car horn sounding once behind him, unlike New York's raucous horn honkers, politely invited him to move on; the lights had gone green.

He hadn't far to go before turning right into Lansdowne Crescent. Weird thoughts cascaded through Billy's mind. It was ten o'clock in the morning, too early to check into the guest house he had booked into on the Carrickfergus Road; he drove slowly on up into the Crescent. It was not how he remembered it. There were bungalows on his right where there used to be

160

green fields. Cresting the incline, he pulled over to the kerb on his left, parked and silenced the car.

Sitting still, staring in front of him, barely breathing, he noticed that the copse of tall elm trees that once adorned the bottom of the Crescent was gone, supplanted by a cluster of dwellings. A residential development covered the fields he had freely roamed as a child. Hidden in seclusion behind the houses on his left was the Sisters of the Cross and Passion convent. Their Order owned Drumalis Estate, which accommodated a large military encampment during the second world war. Billy had good reason to remember the vast colony of Nissan huts that served as billets for the garrison's personnel.

In 1945, when the war ended, the military barracks was decommissioned, with the vacated Nissan huts utilised to provide much needed temporary social housing. Billy's father, a demobilised veteran, was allocated one. Billy didn't know if he was born in their Nissan hut home, but his earliest memory finds him there. The family was rehoused in Sallagh Park when Billy was seven or eight years of age. If Billy had parked on the right side of the road, the hut he was reared in would have been directly facing him. In his mind's eye, he could visualise it. Its circular brownish brick front, brown panelled front door with a narrow vertical steel-framed window on either side and the windows dressed with white net curtains washed so thin they offered little privacy.

The hut was about sixteen feet wide and about thirty-five feet long. Billy remembered stepping it out in a childish way, trying to get some measure of its size. *Why on earth was I doing that?* He didn't know. Maybe it was something said when he had his first birthday party. He was six, and his mother let him have pals from school come to party and play. They had great fun. It was new to some of them; they'd never been inside a Nissan hut be-fore, never mind playing hide and seek among a whole colony of them. Maybe a pal had innocently said, "My house is bigger than yours," or something like that.

A fragment of memory long dormant. Perhaps.

The back end of the Nissan hut was brownish brick too, with a narrow vertical steel-framed window on either side of a rear door. Single sheets of corrugated tin, painted black, formed the curved uninsulated enclosure that was cold in winter. Sometimes condensation on the inner surface froze, forming a thin sheet of glass-like ice. The amenities were basic. They had a stove, in his mind's eye, the brick chimney rearing up above the roof of the hut in front of him, a tin bath, a scullery, sleeping areas separated by blankets hung on wires, and electric lighting consisting of two bulbs dangling from the roof at either end of the hut. There was no hot water; it had to be heated on the stove. The lavatory was outside in a shed-like thing that his birthday party friends found funny too. It was, at best, very basic living. But that's how it was for him, his brother, three sisters, mother and father until they were rehoused among strangers when the Nissan hut commu-nity was scattered, a mini Diaspora. Somehow living in a new estate with all mod cons wasn't the same for Billy. It seemed heartless.

Whether by chance or design, the hut was built on an east-west alignment, which he would later discover was the cause of something that would fascinate him. In early mornings as the seasons changed, the sun's rays rising in the east would pierce the copse of elm trees and beam in through the hut's east-facing windows. The lower the sun's beams, Billy figured out eventu-ally, the further into the hut they stretched, illuminating the in-terior. As the sun rose in the sky, its beams retreated, leaving the hut's interior gloomy. Billy spent hours marching with the sun

162

on its journey inside his Nissan hut home. The morning sun retreating as it moved towards noon also moved to Billy's right. The left side of the hut darkened as the right side brightened before it disappeared altogether, leaving the entire interior drab and lifeless. Billy observed the same process when the sun had moved around to the west, noting that the process reversed and that the sunshine differed in colour and intensity. When his mother asked what he was doing, he would say, "I'm following the sun."

"Billy, you're a wonder son," she would say, wondering, *what'll he get up to next?*

Remembering his Nissan hut home in the middle of a copse of elm trees, Billy felt he was back in a kind of wonderland. His mind skipped momentarily to Thoreau's cabin at Walden Pond. But it was all gone now, like the snow off a ditch in spring, as old folk would often remark about something transient. His humble home was the last to go. It ended its useful life as a scout den before it was demolished and carted away piece by piece, fragment by fragment like bits of transient memory.

The sound of a bell tolling interrupted his thoughts. Smiling, he knew it must be noon. The chapel bell always announced the Angelus prayer at noon. Some things never change. Time to check-in at the guest house, he decided, letting the car roll quietly down to U-turn at the bottom of the Crescent, where he was literally within touching distance of his old home.

The guest house door opened to his knock, revealing a man of little height, beaming from ear to ear, looking up at him with searching mischievous brown eyes that immediately suggested deep reservoirs of wit and humour. He was not a young man; neither was the lady standing behind him, who, as it turned out, was his wife, Vera. Formalities of registration completed Billy shown his room, with the invitation, which he gratefully accepted, to join his hosts for a cup of tea in the lounge when freshened up.

"Let's say in half an hour," his host Harry said, smiling leaving Billy to his unpacking.

His room was spacious and comfortable with a bird's eye view of the townscape far below and thanks to the elevation, he had great WiFi too. Gazing down he could see Drumalis Convent nestling snuggly among the forest of tall trees. His keen eyes traversed the length of Lansdowne Crescent to find the site of his tin hut home.

Billy spent a good half hour taking tea with his hosts and chatting amiably about this and that. Harry, he thought, was a curious little man and not just in the inquisitive sense. But Billy enjoyed dancing to the tune of his mischievous probing. Armed with a few suggestions of what to visit and where he might eat later, Billy left Harry and Vera to head downtown.

Passing the straw-coloured apartment block that had replaced the Latharna Hotel, he counted the uninhabited, ground floor shop fronts begging occupation. There were nine redundant naked glazed shop frontages exhibiting signs of rejection. An undertaker had occupied one, but he had found another resting place. *This is just another example of a development suffering at the hands of town planners imposing conditions that anyone with commercial wit would have recognised as folly,* Billy thought.

Feeling insignificant, Billy crossed to the other side of Main Street to better view the apartment block edifice that had replaced the hotel that had for so long an aura of permanence about it. Impressive, as it was, its underbelly of empty shopfronts conveyed a different impression. Entrance to the apartments was through an electronically operated storey high gate and the parking lot beyond. Like an ascending lift, he raised his eyes slowly upwards to roof level. Black, flat roof sections, projecting over the supporting structure, hung like black-headed crows hovering over a sheep's carcass. He blinked to despatch the image from his thoughts.

In his mind, Billy contrasted the unimposing apartment block frontage with that of the Latharna Hotel with its impressive Georgian facade and expansive entrance leading into a vast high ceilinged foyer. It had been a big solid rich substantial-looking building with huge windows dressed in acres of linen hangings. Many times had he walked through that entrance into the foyer.

Glancing left, he noted that the Tweedy Atcheon Drapery store, its entrance set back from the pavement, entered under a multi-coloured glazed portico, through which the sun tinted the paving below, had also fallen victim to the wrecker's ball. As a child by his mother's side, Billy imagined he was on a magic carpet gliding into the store. Inside, he stood mesmerised as the money trolley overhead on wires whizzed around the store quickly, completing customer's transactions. Looking back, he realised it was pure theatre.

Crossing Main Street, he wondered where the town fathers had put the war memorial making space for the traffic lights. *Something I could ask Harry,* he thought.

Main Street, he remembered growing up as a wide busy avenue. Walking west, it seemed to taper the further he walked, making him feel constricted and squeezed. A thought that he might meet someone he recognised or someone might recognise him struggled in his head for resolution. But he saw not one face he knew. All he met were strangers to him, as he was to them.

The old gasworks site was now a carwash, and what was once McNeill's Hotel now provided sheltered housing. His sister's wedding reception was in Mc Neill's Hotel, and he remembered that occasion with great affection.

As he walked, he searched for a good flower shop and for something to take back to New York as a memento of his visit. Billy had another purpose for the flowers.

But it seemed that Main Street had its fair share of charity shops. People walked about in twos and threes, slowly going about their business, occasionally glancing almost furtively in shop windows. They weren't hesitating or stopping to look; they were like transients killing time, passing through. He remembered a bustling, busy, noisy exciting thoroughfare full of happy people. This was different.

What once was The Kings Arms Hotel was now at street level, a supermarket crowned with nursing home accommodation. He had walked the length of Main Street without finding a decent restaurant. He didn't find a flower shop either but purchased cut flowers from a greengrocer. He didn't know the person who served him or anyone else in the shop.

Standing at the McGarel Town Hall, staring across at the Ulster Bank where he had his first savings account many years ago, he felt a surge of reassurance. Somewhere among the debris of childhood memorabilia in his Manhattan apartment was his Ulster Bank savings deposit book. Smiling, he thought, *I think there might be five pounds still in it. Maybe I'll have some fun when I return to New York, trying to reclaim it with interest.* Strange, he thought how fragments of memory need little encouragement to colour the present.

Turning left down Cross Street, he found the eateries Harry had suggested, but his walk on Main Street had dulled his appetite. Cross Street, strangely quiet on Saturday afternoon, bemused him. It used to be a thriving, busy, bustling street; now, it was lifeless, dead. Walking on, he realised why. The biggest greengrocery in the town was gone. It was always busy, full of colour, with men busy weighing, counting and shouting out to customers what was good today. It poured itself onto the street with stalls full of bananas, oranges, apples, nuts, melons, vegetables, peas, beans, plums and heaps of other things. It was for Billy growing up, a menagerie of delicious desirable foods. The ambience was impromptu, infectious, fun, pure street theatre. Something Goldsmith wrote about the Kingfisher a long time ago flashed into his mind, 'Innocently to amuse the imagination in this dream of life is wisdom.'

How insightful is that? He thought

The Savoy cinema purveyor of dreams captured on celluloid for patrons of all ages with imagination, or none, was gone too. Billy had fond memories of the Savoy and the double seats in the back row of the balcony. But that's a different story. The beating heart of the street had been ripped out and shredded.

He turned right onto Dunluce Street with the expectation of butchers, bakers, greengrocers, hardware merchants, fishmongers, cobblers and other small businesses plying their trade. There was nothing. The once-thriving street was grim, lonely and all but abandoned. This part of town felt lonelier, bleak, deserted. Billy didn't linger.

Turning left onto High Street, he stood under the shadow of the high rise apartment buildings that dominated the townscape he had seen on his way into town. They rehoused many residents of the old town. Not before their time, some would say. He had grown up with folk reared in the little whitewashed stone houses linked by the network of lanes that knitted the community together. He thought, *decent people* as he wandered over the bridge under which the Inver River flowed, searching for the sea. On the centre of the bridge, he paused. Familiar odours teased his nose. He sniffed the air like a hound seeking its quarry. He felt his appetite returning. Noise from Inver Park reminded him that it was Saturday afternoon; a football match was in progress.

Turning left onto Station Road, smell, taste, desire and location coalesced. The Station Road Chip Shop. It was still there. What a delightful surprise! The smell of fish and chips was seductive. He couldn't resist it. Billy had to go in. The booths he and his pals had sat in, eating fish and chips after football matches, were still there; nothing had changed. He ordered a fish supper at the counter, with tea bread and butter, paid for his meal, and sat waiting in the same booth he had sat in decades ago. Billy was excitedly hungry. Seated against the back wall beside the ornate fireplace, he had an unobstructed view of the chip shop cooking and serving area. A steady stream of folk, all shapes and sizes, entered and collected their takeaways. He was the only person eating in until a shabbily dressed middle-aged red-eyed man shuffled in and settled in an opposite booth facing Billy. *He's been drinking since he woke up,* Billy thought, watching as the man studied the menu with great intent, running his shaking hand several times down the listings. Reaching into a ragged coat pocket, he took out a brown paper bag and tipped a spill of coins of little value onto the table. Separating them by denomination into small piles, he calculated his accumulated wealth. That done, the man perused the menu studiously again. The waitress arriving at his side asked, "The usual Willie?"

"Aye," he muttered.

That, in a word, was the difference perhaps between what he might have ordered if he could have afforded it and what he could afford.

Billy's food arrived. The waitress placed the cutlery and napkin on the table and, between the knife and fork, set a plate with two pieces of battered cod and a heap of chips. To the side, she put bread, butter, mushy peas and tea. The smell when the brown vinegar sizzled on the chips and fish funnelled up Billy's nostrils like a runaway train. He set to and attacked his meal with relish.

He avoided eye contact with the gentleman opposite as he ate but couldn't resist glancing across when the waitress served him, curious to see what his usual was. The usual, it turned was a small plate of chips, a child's portion and a cup of tea. Billy noted the few coins the man had left as he carefully put them back into his paper bag. He felt sorry for him so much, so he considered leaving a couple of pounds on his table as he left. Then a notion occurred to him that the poor man might be insulted; he might not be poor, and maybe he likes being the way he is. In the end, he thought, *if I give him something, he'd most likely go next door to the Royal Bar and drink it.* It was then that he realised his foolishness. The Royal Bar wasn't there anymore; the wreckers ball had taken care of it too. *Impulse and choice unhelpful companions invite complications,* Billy reminded himself.

As football fans trickled in after the match and occupied the booths, Billy left the chip shop and headed down Station Road. It hadn't changed much. According to the posters on the locked gates, the market yard that had once served livestock markets now hosted market traders and other community events. The railway station that gave the street its name was gone. Moved east about a mile or so to make room for road improvements. He had seen the new station driving into town. At the bottom of the street, he turned left and walked alongside the new dual carriageway heading back to town on what remained of Circular Road.

Deep within himself, Billy felt an irresistible need to walk the length of Lansdowne Crescent, end-to-end, before returning to the guest house on the Carrickfergus Road. Slowly at a measured pace, he walked back through the years one step at a time. Pausing at the bottom of the Crescent, he stood and stared through a gap in the hedge at the exact spot where his Nissan hut home had been. It was a back garden now. He could see a swing gently swaying to and fro as if hastily left by a child called in for lunch, a slide and other bits and pieces of children's playthings. We didn't have any of those, Billy thought, but then we didn't need them.

He remembered how the curved shape of the hut substantially reduced the usable floor area. His father was forever banging his head on it, and ordinary pieces of rectangular furniture didn't fit very well either. But he was happy there. How long he stood letting rivers of thought flood his mind, he didn't know. His mind had drifted away again to Thoreau's cabin at Walden Pond. A car door banging up the Crescent abruptly interrupted his daydreaming. Billy turned, retracing his steps past the string of bungalows that weren't there when he was a boy. For a weird moment, he wondered why he had a bunch of flowers in his hand. Realising it was too late to put them to their intended use, Billy left them in the boot of his car lest Harry and Vera got the wrong idea.

Feeling tired, he hoped to make it to his room without engaging anyone entering the guesthouse. But, as it turned out, it was his good fortune that the ever-alert diminutive attentive Harry met him in the hallway before his foot made it onto the first tread of the stairs, with the kind offer of a welcome drink in the lounge. Billy couldn't refuse, but he wasn't looking forward to dancing the curiosity waltz again with Harry.

"What's your tipple?" Harry asked. "I've Scotch, Irish, and Gin?"

"A Jameson, please if you have it."

"A good choice, Sir and indeed I do have it," Harry said, pouring Billy a generous measure.

"And what would you like with it, water or something?"

"It's fine just the way it is," Billy responded, watching Harry helping himself to a large Bombay gin and a mere touch of tonic.

Settled with their drinks, Harry was entertainingly chatty, so much so that the thought crossed Billy's mind that, perhaps, he'd been to Bombay earlier in the day.

Billy spent a very relaxing couple of hours with Harry chatting. He told Harry where he had walked, what he had seen, omitting to mention his fish and chips meal, commenting in passing on the dilapidated state of parts of the town. Knowing exactly where Billy was talking about, Harry set about telling him the whys and the wherefores of it all. In summary, the offending areas were part of a town centre development plan that took longer to implement than at first thought. After sharing another drink with Harry, Billy reluctantly took his leave and retired to his room for the evening.

It had been a long day. Billy was tired. Refreshed after a hot shower, he settled to read the book he always carried with him on his travels; Henry David Thoreau's book, Walden. Setting the book aside, he tried to sleep, but sleep didn't come easily. He had read Thoreau's book several times and liked it because it was a fascinating read. The question forming in his mind was, *why does it travel with me all the time?*

Thoreau had built a cabin in woodland near Walden Pond and lived there for two years, pursuing a life of self-reliance and simplicity. Billy put the bedside light on, reached for the book, found the page he wanted and reread Thoreau's words for the umpteenth time.

'I went to the woods because I wished to live deliberately, to front only the essential facts of life, and see if I could not learn what it was it had to

teach, and not, when I came to die, discover that I had not lived. I did not wish to live what was not life, living is so dear; nor did I wish to practice resignation, unless it was quite necessary. I wanted to.................. get to the whole meanness of it, and publish its meanness to the world; or if it were sublime, to know it by experience, and be able to give a true account of it in my next excursion.'

He knew that Thoreau's undertaking was an experiment of fixed duration, not a life. To fully know and understand the meanness of life, one had to live it, all of it, not dabble in it. Then he saw the connections; the huts, the woods, simplicity, hand to mouth existence, self-reliance and poverty. Thoreau shaped and lived his experiment, but for Billy, life in the colony of Nissan huts where he grew up wasn't an experiment; it was real, every day a raw reality. His demobbed father, a tradesman, couldn't find work while unskilled non-service folk could. He remembered then a conversation when his father, speaking of where his family was living, said, "Life's carved out for the likes of us by others. Carve out your own life son; it's up to you." Words from Carew's poem, *The Pretensions of Poverty*, ricocheted around in his head:

'Thou dost presume too much, poor needy wretch,

To claim a station in the firmament

Because thy humble cottage, or thy tub,

Nurses some lazy or pedantic virtue.'

For Billy, there was nothing romantic or virtuous about being poor and needy. Life for his family was all about surviving, hand to mouth, day by day, every day. As his father reminded him, "others craved it out for us, son." Slowly he set the book down, knowing he had read it for the last time.

Breakfast was available from 8 am to 10 am on Sundays. There were three fellow guests in the small breakfast room when

172

Billy joined them shortly after 8 am. A young couple occupied a table for two, and a middle-aged woman sat at a table at the other end of the room. Billy thought of the Greta Garbo remark 'I want to be alone' and smiled. His 'good morning' greeting on entering received smiling responses from the young couple. The middle-aged woman looked him up and down over the top of her steel-rimmed glasses as a farmer at a market would appraise cattle. She acknowledged his greeting with a curt nod of her head and resumed her breakfast.

The room had a friendly, informal, welcoming feel about it. Along one wall, a selection of foods and beverages was available for those preferring a continental type breakfast. Billy helped himself to orange juice, found a table with a view and sat down. He was lost in thought, gazing down on the streetscape of his childhood, spread out way below him, when he sensed a presence by his side. Turning his head, he found himself looking into the pair of bright brown eyes that greeted him last evening. This morning his host Harry, the man of little height, was waiting on him, dressed as an Italian waiter, immaculately turned out in black trousers, white shirt open at the neck, sleeves buttoned at the wrists. Formality was the name of the game, and Billy knew how to play it. Having ordered the cooked breakfast, he wanted to know what a full Ulster was. Harry answered his question with panache and, remaining in character, asked, "How would you like your eggs, Sir? Sunny-side-up?"

"Yes, please," Billy said, stifling a laugh.

"Won't be long, Sir," his host-cum-waiter assured him, departing with a flourish.

When his breakfast was presented, Billy suppressed a gasp as aromas of home invaded his senses. Two sunny-side-up eggs smiled at him, accompanied by two beef sausages, two rashers of back bacon, two tomatoes halved and pan-fried, black pudding, potato and soda bread, and a rack of toasted wheaten bread, with condiments.

In his hut home at the foot of the Crescent, an egg and bacon breakfast was an occasion for celebration.

"Anything else I can get you, Sir?" his waiter come host inquired as he poured Billy coffee.

"Thank you. No, I think I have more than enough," Billy gratefully acknowledged as he set about demolishing his substantial breakfast.

Enjoying his third coffee alone in the breakfast room, Billy hardly noticed his breakfast debris being cleared away until his waiter, now genial host, asked, "Any plans for today?"

Billy, for no particular reason, responded vaguely. "A long walk might be the best thing after that huge breakfast. Don't you think?"

"Did you find somewhere to eat yesterday?" his host continued.

"Indeed I did, thank you," Billy said, hoping that he hadn't filled his bedroom with the smell of fish and chips.

Sensing that his host was settling for a long chat, Billy excused himself and returned to his room.

Why did I do that? He wondered. *Why am I always hiding my background?* Billy knew perfectly well why. There's nothing wrong or to be ashamed about being reared in a hut; he reminded himself, he knew that. He just had no time for background probers who measured ability by the metric of social class, school or university.

Camera and other bits and pieces in his shouldered rucksack Billy set off on his walk. He had decided before he even left New York what his route would be. As he approached Main Street and Curran Road junction, the south side of the Methodist

174

Church was almost in touching distance. This building, built in 1884 with hand-sculpted sandstone blocks laid with the precision of master builders, he loved. It filled its confined site but never looked quashed, squeezed or out of place. Its small side and front bordered lawns a testament to loving care. Turning right onto Curran Road, he paused to admire the front of the church. There was nothing pretentious about it; it was solidly simply Methodist. The church was closed. It was too early for Sunday service. *Hard to believe the Methodists have been giving witness here for nearly a hundred and twenty years,* Billy thought.

There was a vacant lot where the Regal Cinema had been before it fell to the wrecker's ball. Was it Art Nouveau or Art Deco? He couldn't decide, but its image was riveted into his mind? The Saturday afternoon matinees; Roy Rodgers and Trigger, The Three Stooges, Robin Hood and his merry men, Spencer Tracy dragging his foot behind him and Frankenstein. He had to scrape together pennies all week to afford the cost of admission, collecting and selling jam jars. As thoughts tumbled around in his head, he realised what he was doing out of necessity back then was what society is doing now; recycling. The notion made him smile.

But there was a way to get into the cinema without paying. It needed teamwork, coordination and timing. A service entrance to the Regal Cinema off Circular Road also served as the emergency exit if needed from the pit area, i.e. the cheap seats. The pit area was all Billy, and his pals could afford. The emergency exit route from the pit area also served toilets. Often when cash strapped, they would pitch in what pennies they had to get enough money for one or two comrades to gain admission on the understanding that once in, they would visit the toilets and open the emergency exit door to let their pals sneak in. The trick was never to re-enter as a group; otherwise, they would be caught and ejected. Patience was the name of the game. It was great fun, spoiled or foiled; however one looked at it now. Looking back, he thought they'd put the emergency exit doors to an innovative use by creating an emergency access. To miss a Saturday afternoon matinee for want of a few pennies was for Billy and pals a disaster to be averted at any cost.

Curran Road was quiet, and Billy didn't meet anyone as he strolled along. Not much had changed on this road that had its unique place in history. The police barracks, blind-sided by the gunrunners in 1914, now offered residential accommodation, without barred windows, of course. Billy wondered what ghosts if any, that building harboured?

Approaching what was once the Curran Road entrance to the Drumalis Estate, his heart beat a little faster. From a distance, he saw the tall black painted cast iron railings proudly standing erect on a low granite stone plinth topped with dressed sandstone copings. Holding his breath, he walked slowly until he stood in front of what used to be the gated entrance to the colony of forty to fifty Nissan huts on the Drumalis Estate. The street name told him that Corran Manor was the new housing estate that subsequently replaced the colony. The retained concave pillared railings that marked the boundary of Drumalis Estate formed an impressive entrance to the well-beaten lane; he had trudged on his way to and from school as a child. Something in his mind didn't quite fit. The pillars that supported the huge gates were too far apart. The two pedestrian gates and their supporting pillars were missing; that's why what he was looking at didn't fit the picture in his mind. The little gate lodge was gone too. It had sat snugly on the right side of the lane behind the railings. In school, learning to write with pen and ink, he thought of the little gate lodge each time he dipped his pen into the inkpot on his desk. It was small, almost petite, single-story, built with dressed granite stone and hipped slate roof. It must have been the chimney perched on the top that made him think of it as an inkpot. The front door and windows on either side were framed with red brick, and the woodwork painted a bluish-grey. The external quoined corners of the lodge added definition, solidity and quality. Drawing back from the gate lodge, he looked closely at the square sandstone sentinel pillars topped with ornate pyramid-shaped capstones symmetrically in harmony with the hipped roof of the lodge. It was the attention to detail that he was seeing and admiring for the first time. Billy, so lost in thought, didn't notice the dog walker passing in front of him.

He remembered something else about the gate lodge. It was the sound of music. Sometimes he stopped to listen to the piano or someone singing; other times, he didn't listen. Why not? *Probably it didn't sound that good to his uncultured ear,* he thought. Later he would learn that the lady who lived there taught music.

Slipping back in time, he was the little boy going home. A scruffy-looking ill-clad little boy wearing hand me down clothes and footwear. Patched short pants were no disgrace for everyday use. On Sundays, church days, he had to wear his best. Billy, boyishly dragging his feet shuffling up the gentle gradient into Corran Manor, didn't see the dwellings stretching before him. He was moving slowly, threading his way home again through the elm trees, passing around, and cutting in between neighbours' huts towards his own. He stopped where he knew his hut had been. Billy was standing in front of a neatly gardened bungalow looking up Lansdowne Crescent, through the hedge, past where he stood yesterday looking in. A bungalow with its big picture window, Venetian blinds closed, and paved driveway stood where his home had sat, ringed by a pathetic string of rough paving slabs. Other tin huts were splayed to the right and left of his.

He could see the east end of the cylindrical hut, lengthwise segmented resting on the concrete slab prepared for it in his mind's eye. He could hear the birds still feeding their young in early summer, readying to fledge and the trees, elm, chestnut, oak, ash, birch and others fully clothed in their summer foliage. He remembered the ground around the huts and trees carpeted with foxgloves, primroses and other flowering plants. Squinting through the trees at his home, the vision of summer eased through autumn into winter. There was no bird song. The trees yielding to photosynthesis displayed their autumnal colours of browns, yellows, gold, and bronze. He remembered the fun they had, boys and girls among the fallen leaves. It snowed most winters then. They fought their snowball wars with enthusiasm in and around the colony of huts and forest of trees. Then it was spring again, signalled by the arrival of snowdrops, daffodils and other plants eager for a breath of fresh air. Profoundly sighing, Billy thanked God; they were not sealed in as children or sealed off as families from each other like those living in New York. Billy never felt lonely as a child but often felt alone in New York.

Staring at his truncated home, Billy saw it as a tube, the cylinder in which family values were shared and daily passed on in the everyday mundane tasks of living. The habits, customs, religious and other family practices formed in his tin hut home was the bedrock of support that sustained Billy all his life. But it was much more; it was the conduit that channelled his energies towards improving his lot in life.

"Carve a life for yourself, son," was his father's mantra.

He had, and some might have said, pulled himself up by his bootstraps.

The Venetian blind on the big picture window flicking open interrupted his daydreaming. The woman staring out disturbed him. He looked away uncomfortable, disconcerted, embarrassed, unsure of himself about to walk away when she appeared in her driveway asking,

"Are you alright? Are you lost?"

"No, thank you, no, I used to live here, that's all," he somehow managed to mutter. He saw her looking at him oddly.

"We've always lived here," she said. "We bought the house when it was built; no one but us has ever lived here."

"Sorry," he apologised. "I didn't mean that I lived in your house. I lived here before your house was built," he offered, hoping to dispel her confusion but only in the process of adding to it.

"There were no houses here before ours was built," she replied, raising her arms in a gesture of exasperation.

"You're right," Billy said, trying to assuage the woman's frustration. "Before your house was built, there was a scout den there. You didn't know that, I suppose?"

"No…I didn't."

"And way before that," Billy continued, "there were other buildings too. It's all a long time ago. That's when I lived here. I'm in town for a brief visit and thought I'd have a look-see. I'm very sorry if I've intruded. I wasn't looking at your house, I was remembering something else. Please accept my apologies."

The woman of no name, no description, graciously accepted Billy's apologies.

Parting, he set about exploring the rest of Corran Manor Estate. Corran Manor road twisted and turned as it made its way upwards branching off, to form a 'Y' junction. Fully aware now of the consequences of standing staring at somebody's house while musing about the patchwork colony of Nissan huts that once spread over the whole area, stretching down to the sea, Billy cautiously moved on. *What freedom and fun he and his boyhood pals had cavorting and getting up to all sorts of devilment around here.* He thought.

It was a pleasant, quiet Sunday morning walk. Raised living room blinds afforded him furtive glimpses of comfortable, peaceful interiors, photographs on piano tops, mantelpieces, wall hung mirrors and paintings; people at home moving about their business. Billy kept a tight rein on his inquisitive glancing lest residents interpreted his behaviour as voyeuristic. Across the road, a man washed his car. Behind him, somewhere, a lawnmower came to life. The tall mature trees in Drumalis, silent sentinels, watched over all as he wandered around. Where Corran Manor Estate ended, Billy stood and looked out over the sea. It was very familiar territory to him, as a child on his way in summer, towel in hand with pals to the bathing boxes dotted on the promenade below. Looking around, he tried to figure out where the communal hut had been. It was the wash house, laundry some might have called it.

Then something caught his eye in a back garden. It was a sunken fire pit that people could sit around in the evening and spit roast or barbecue food. Another must-have fad perhaps to impress the neighbours. But it reminded him of Christmas among the trees and Nissan huts. Especially the Christmas it snowed. Big snowflakes drifted down, slowly settling on the tree branches bending them to their will.

It was a bright starry Christmas Eve night. The planning and preparations were readied. Braziers, discarded when the military encampment closed, were collected and placed in a five-pointed star configuration in the middle of the colony of Nissan huts, where the Curran Manor road split, forming two avenues. Frost's poem; *The Road Not Taken*, leapt into Billy's mind;

'Two roads diverged in a yellow wood,
And sorry I could not travel both

And be one traveller, long I stood
And looked down one as far I could
To where it bent in the undergrowth.'

The wood in his mind wasn't yellow. Snow coloured the trees and undergrowth white. The braziers could have been used as beacons of some sort or even landing strip lighting for aircraft. *Not among trees, Billy,* he told himself. They were often used for street lighting, except there weren't any streets; little beaten tracks served the colony of huts. On Christmas Eve, children filled the braziers with dry wood they gathered among the trees. At 11.45 pm, each family left their home in candlelight procession, footprinting the virgin snow to the ring of braziers, lit by the candle bearers on the first stroke of midnight. The flaming wood incensing the night air created a feathery primrose coloured glow that rose and spread over *the gathering.* The cold night air quickly cooled the rising coloured smoke until it lost its buoyancy and, hanging motionless, veiled *the gathering.* It was a moment of awe.

A female voice sounded a note, carol singing commenced, voices rose and fell in unison, expertly guided by the music teacher from the gate lodge. They sang until the brazier fires burned low and then processioned back to their huts. Beyond the glow of the fire, the trees kept silent watch.

Billy had experienced many memorable occasions. He was there when Pavarotti sang in Central Park and thought it was fantastic. But he had never forgotten the Christmas Eve when the Nissan hut colony of families sang carols impromptu among the snow-laden trees under a starry sky. He knew that nothing could ever beat that experience. In their hut, hot drinks in hand, Billy and family shared Christmas joy.

Sighing, he turned and strolled back out of Corran Manor onto the Curran Road. I wonder, he thought, *will the children growing up here have the same freedom as I had?* He doubted it. *Will this community of families be like our colony?* He wondered. But he liked the estate; it wasn't bare of trees and felt friendly. I could live here; he thought and promptly thought no more about it.

Pausing at the Curran Court Hotel, thinking about lunch, he was about to turn left onto Tower Road when he noticed that the waste ground across the road was now a bowling green and park. With time on his side and at ease with himself, he crossed the road for a look-see. Entering the park, he couldn't miss the impressive sculpture erected in memory of the first Ulster Emigrants who sailed from Larne in May 1717 on the "Friends Goodwill" bound for Boston. They were to be the first of many, the inscription said. *I followed in their footsteps two and a half centuries later,* Billy thought, *only I flew.*

As he wandered around the park, thoughts caressing in his head, Billy did a couple of circuits before leaving and walking up Tower Road. He walked up the pavement tracing the fingers of his left hand along the remnant of the granite stone wall that once had delineated the Drumalis Estate. It felt strangely warm to his touch, friendly and welcoming. Cresting Tower Road, he paused and looked down on the sparkling blue seascape before him, drinking it all in, absorbing the moment. On his right, the Bay Field was as he remembered it, vast, expansive, inviting and challenging, especially on Saturday mornings when he had to pull on a shirt, turn out for his team and play a match. But it was fun.

He noted the leisure centre at the bottom of Tower Road, where it met the promenade, built on land once part of Drumalis Estate. It wasn't there in his time. In those days, young and some not so young swam in the sea. Walking north, it took a moment or two before he realised that the red brick bathing boxes and their elevated planked piers that stretched boldly out into the sea were gone. *That's a shame,* he thought. Protruding above the ebbing tide, he could see the stumps of the cast-iron columns that once supported the planked route along the length of the piers to the diving boards perched high above the ocean. The hours he and his pals had spent diving, swimming and having fun in the sea surged through his mind like a mini tsunami. They had ordered their summer days in keeping with the ebb and flow of the tides. The routine was simple, play football in the Town Park until the tide was full in, then gallop out of the park, down to the bathing box at the foot of the snake path, a quick change into togs, and a mad dash along the pier swallow diving into the welcoming sea. As he strolled along the promenade towards the winding path, he took a moment to persuade himself that he wasn't daydreaming again.

As a child, the upward winding steep snake path never intimidated him. He often ran up it. Now several feet taller than he was then, it challenged him, but there were a few more years on his clock now. He wondered for a moment if he could make it to the top, knowing for sure that he wouldn't be running. Slowly he paced upwards, paused midway for a breather, turned and admired the view that had shaped his childhood. Away to his right, the lonesome sightless Chaine Tower looked out over the sea and beyond on the fairways of Larne Golf Club on Islandmagee; he could see the miniature golfers about their play. Panning left the Maidens topping the Hullin Rocks hove into sight and beyond them, the Mull of Kintyre proudly pointing across the North Channel to Ulster. The full circle completed; taking a deep breath, Billy continued his climb to the summit. At the entrance to the Town Park, he paused again. Looking around, he wondered if he would ever, beyond the realms of imagination, see it again.

The park had changed. The goalposts were gone. The pitch he and his pals had played on bore 'keep off the grass' warning signs. A few people, slinging balls about for dogs to chase, ignored the signs. The children's park he had played as a child had been replaced with a much better children's play and activity area, and he observed many were making good use of it. He remembered the children's play area swings chained up and planks of wood set into slides to prevent their use on Sundays. That was a long time ago. Now different attitudes prevailed. New all-weather surfaces invited all sorts of ball games, including tennis and football. On the whole, the park he thought was very much better than it was.

Leaving the park by the Bankhead Lane, he turned left onto the Glenarm Road making his way back to the carpark on Narrow Gauge Road. He hadn't forgotten the flowers in the trunk of his car. Time to put them to their intended use, Billy thought, making his way to the town cemetery in Craigyhill where his parents rested. Outside the lower gate, he parked up, retrieved the flowers and made his way to his parents grave. Billy paid for the grave to be maintained and, standing head respectfully bowed, was satisfied that it was. Laying his flowers against the headstone, he prayed that his mother and father found their eternal reward, which they richly deserved in his view. How could they not? He asked himself. The little Yew tree he had planted was little no more, but carefully pruned served as a constant reminder of the brevity of human life.

Billy spent quite a bit of time with his parents in reflection before he reluctantly took his leave. He began to feel surprisingly hungry as he drove along the Coast Road towards the Londonderry Arms Hotel in Carnlough for lunch. The hotel was busy but found him a table in a small overflow but comfortable dining room. He had a view across the room from his table, through a small window, of a young chestnut tree in full leaf ruffling in the gentle onshore breeze.

Billy didn't need the menu the waitress offered; he had already decided on the traditional dish of County Antrim boiled potatoes served in their jackets with boiled shredded cabbage sautéed in the juices of and served with thick-cut back bacon. He never liked the streaky bacon served in New York. Asked if he wanted something to drink, he settled for water, tap water. It wasn't long before the waitress returned with a serving trolley from which she produced his warm plate and placed four rashers of thick-cut bacon on it, followed with floury jacketed potatoes and piping hot cabbage topped with knobs of slowly melting butter. Spuds, butter, cabbage and a bit of decent bacon was all that Billy's heart was set on, and he fell to tackling it with enthusiasm.

It was late afternoon when Billy left the hotel and headed back to town. The on-shore breeze gentle added white tops to the incoming waves. He was in no hurry back but soon found himself in a convoy of day-trippers in less of a hurry than he was. Billy settled, enjoyed the experience and before he realised he was turning into Lansdowne Crescent. The tall native trees in Drumalis behind the houses on his left seemed to be sadly waving goodbye. Billy, he thought, *your imagination is running away with you.* At the bottom of the Crescent, within touching distance of where his Nissan hut home used to be, his imagination would have taken flight had he not reined it in. Something was nagging at Billy, but hard as he tried, he couldn't discern what it was. Sauntering back to the guest house, pondering his thoughts, he noticed a property on the other side of the road with a for sale board planted in the garden. Wrong side of the road for me and too far away from…what? If it had been the bungalow next door to where the Nissan hut had been, it might have piqued his interest. But it wasn't, and that was that Billy thought.

It was early evening when Billy let himself into the guesthouse. Harry, the ever-alert gatekeeper always on duty, welcomed him warmly with the offer of more generous hospitality. Billy, though he didn't admit it, had found his day more than tiring. As they chatted amiably, Harry coloured in verbally some detail around the landscape of Billy's day. Billy omitted to mention his visit to the cemetery. He was still hiding his background, trying to understand why, with a growing suspicion that perhaps Harry knew more about him than his smiling eyes revealed. In the end, it didn't matter to Billy. His short visit was over; he was leaving early in the morning, and that was that. So he thought.

It had gone past seven o'clock when he settled up with Harry and Vera. Paid cash, pocketed his receipt, declined the offer of a takeaway breakfast box for his journey and said goodnight and goodbye with gratitude. In his room, he packed his small holdall bag, set his alarm, placed Thoreau's book on the bedside table for someone else to enjoy, and wrote a note to Harry and Vera on top of which he placed his unopened bottle of duty-free Jameson whisky. Lights out, he settled to sleep, but sleep didn't come easily. There was light in the early morning sky when Billy slipped quietly out of the guesthouse on the Carrickfergus Road and headed back to New York.

It was evening; Billy stood in his apartment twenty stories up in the sky, looking towards neon illuminated Broadway below. His mind, a confusion of thoughts, was like a millpond mercilessly bombarded by a continuous downpour of malignant raindrops. Perched on high, looking down, he wondered, *who knows what goes on in people's heads? Was his walk among the colony of Nissan huts a daydream? Had he sleepwalked through his entire adult life, drawn down the blinds on his childhood?* So ended the first evening of Billy's return from where he was to where he is now.

The night set in. In bed in his spacious, well-appointed apartment, behind his closed eyes, thoughts of home flashed back and forth like Morse lanterns sending their messages. Images of his mother, father, sisters and brother living in their Nissan hut, the sounds, smells, the simple food, the tiffs, and disagreements coloured his perceptions. He felt a window was opening. His Nissan hut life was life within a life. Memory, an instant, a scene, an act, he debated with himself was something he gathered and processed to tell the story he wanted to believe. The weight of memory on his chest was getting heavier. When they banged the lid of his mother's coffin shut, he bolted upright in bed in a cold sweat. Breathing deeply, he saw her smoothing ruffled feathers when things in the hut turned fractious. He watched her polishing with loving care the bits and pieces of worthless furniture she cherished.

The daydream was the prelude to a fierce attack of homesickness. It was a vicious attack because, for Billy, there could be only one place to be homesick for.

Wide awake, now coffee in hand, he stood at his window up in the sky and looked down on the city that never sleeps. It was alien to him, not unfamiliar; he was alien to it. Billy didn't want to be there…anymore. It was a harsh, cruel, dog eat dog city. But he knew that already; it was just that suddenly he'd had enough.

He pondered for a moment what he would say to the one or two real friends he had in New York. Frost rescued Billy,

'I shall be telling this with a sigh
Somewhere ages and ages hence;
Two roads diverged in a wood and I-

I'll take the road less travelled, and that will make all the difference in my world, he thought. I'll tell them I'm going home; they'll understand that I've made the right choice – for me.

That night he slept like a baby.

Acknowledgements

Reflecting on my life I realise that there is much to be grateful for – even those lived experiences I wouldn't wish on another. I am much indebted to my primary school education in the 1940s for shaping the direction my life would eventually take. It was there that I first encountered Shakespeare, read Macbeth, learned the speeches that I can still recite without much revision. The classroom was a theatre full of drama of all sorts - not just among the children – and much that would be unacceptable today for good or ill.

In college, good-intentioned teachers continued to nurture my interest in the arts – even though they may have been unaware that their efforts were worthwhile. Like many young lads, football occupied most of my headspace at the time. Today I am grateful that seeds sown many decades ago waited patiently, while I was busy in life, for their moment of germination.

During all the pressured years of parenting and providing, I found great friendship, joy and fulfilment in the community of Saint MacNissi's Choral Society and later the same camaraderie with Larne Drama Circle. Treading the boards with them allowed me to relax, let off steam, remember playfulness and stand in others' shoes to look at life through a different prism. Seasons of refreshment and rejuvenation. I gained insights into the dedication and professionalism of the behind the scenes people who willingly and generously shared their talents and expertise. It takes teamwork, which is rarely as easy as the finished product would have the observer believe.

In the chorus line or just one of the crowd, I had time to observe and appreciate the rigour and attention to detail brought to bear on every aspect of production. It was a learned behaviour that I greatly benefited from in my career. I am forever grateful to Fr. E. O'Brien, Bertie Fulton, Beth Duffin, Jay Alexander, Billy Burns and Alison Stewart.

With marriage, children and my career demanding greater attention, writing and performing were relegated to the back seat. It was that or golf and golf won for a few years because I convinced myself I needed fresh air.

Retirement – that time of transition and of taking stock – has seen me return to the classroom again. There is no one more surprised than me to find that this is my 3rd book of short stories. My mother would have said, 'Never knew you had it in you son.' Neither did I.

Crossing over from writing nonfiction to writing, fiction was for me an enormous challenge. Academic writing is about philosophising, pushing the boundaries of knowledge. It is critical and needs to be for sound science. It is impersonal. Fiction is personal. It demands compassion, honesty and a willingness to occupy spaces you would rather not be in. To share feelings.

Without the encouragement of many friends, my crossover would have been even more difficult. There is a hidden richness in every person we encounter. Often our thinking divides us, but our feelings and empathy draw us together. When hearts speak we listen.

I would like to thank all my Larne Drama Circle friends, especially Margaret Stewart, who encouraged my scribbling, and Jim McCarlie who, in many conversations, shaped the content of this book.

I must thank my wonderful wife Annette and family who have contributed so much to my endeavours.

I thank Ian Hooper, Executive Director at Leschenault Press, for diligently guiding and supporting me in the production of this book.

About the Author

Jim shields was born on the Mill brae, Larne, Northern Ireland in 1943. His schooling began in the Mc Kenna Memorial Primary School and continued in Larne Technical College. On completion of his apprenticeship in the construction industry he pursued further education, taking night classes to obtain professional and academic accreditations.

He completed his MSc in Fire Safety Engineering at the University of Edinburgh, followed by his PhD in the same discipline at The University of Ulster.

Jim, Emeritus Professor of Fire Safety Engineering, retired from his academic career in 2004.

A passionate supporter of the arts he was a relative latecomer to creative writing, but once started he has striven to make up for lost time. *Seasons of Affection* is his third published collection of short stories. He has no intention of it being his last.

Other works by Jim:

Scene through a Rearview Mirror – 2019

Naked Widows – 2020

Jim and his wife Annette still live in Larne where they regularly entertain their five children and five grandchildren.